MONSTER JUICE

Fear the Barfitron

GROSSET & DUNLAP
Published by the Penguin Group
Penguin Group (USA) Inc., 375 Hudson Street, New York, New York 10014, USA

USA | Canada | UK | Ireland | Australia | New Zealand | India | South Africa | China
Penguin Books Ltd, Registered Offices: 80 Strand, London WC2R 0RL, England

For more information about the Penguin Group visit penguin.com

Cover illustrated by Amanda Dockery

Library of Congress Cataloging-in-Publication Data is available.

ISBN 978-0-448-46226-4   10 9 8 7 6 5 4 3 2 1

ALWAYS LEARNING   **PEARSON**

To Lady Payne and
our little monster, Molly

Fear the Barfitron

by M. D. Payne

Grosset & Dunlap
An Imprint of Penguin Group (USA) Inc.

Prologue

Three mysterious figures sprinted through a dark, overgrown forest.

"We must be swift," a well-dressed pale man in the lead yelled. "We mustn't risk Percy's safety much longer!"

"We're close," a short woman in a white uniform and a hairnet yelled back. "The boy's house eez just past the creek." She struggled to push along a man nearly twice her size. His sprint slowed to a stumble. Something was wrong. He appeared to be sick, or even worse—wounded.

"Meeee wwwaaa," moaned Percy through his crooked black teeth. "Wwwant go hoooome!"

"Soon, old friend," the well-dressed man gasped. "We just need you to do one thing."

All three jumped into the creek, pushing through the cold, sandy water. Their shoes and pants legs quickly became drenched, but they had to keep moving. Percy wouldn't survive another attack.

Halfway across, the hairnetted woman lost her footing. "*Ay Dios mío!*" she yelped as she slipped face-first into the icy water.

"I've got you," the well-dressed man yelled, and helped her to her feet.

Rising out of the creek, the hairnetted woman didn't even notice the freezing-cold uniform that now clung to her. All she could do was scan the darkness for their friend.

"Percy!" she yelled. "Percy!!!"

Slumped on a log at the edge of the water sat Percy. His huge head slouched over his wide, lifeless chest. They couldn't see Percy's eye, but both were almost sure it must be closed.

"We have to wake him!" the well-dressed man yelled.

They both shot out of the water toward Percy.

And that's when they heard them . . .

Loud, slurpy growls coming from the other side of the creek.

They both froze.

Turning, the well-dressed man's eyes widened in fear. Coming toward them, through the darkness, were dozens—maybe hundreds—of spitting and screeching mouths. More than either of them had ever seen in their lives.

He grabbed Percy's wrinkled face and lifted up his head. Percy's eye popped open in surprise.

"Percy!" he yelled. "They're here. We must run. Now, Percy."

"NOW!" The well-dressed man and woman yelled together.

Percy jumped up, using what life he had left, and the three ran even faster now. Behind them, the sound of the vile creatures was deafening.

"Eet's just up ahead," said the hairnetted woman over the hungry screeching. "Soon after the clearing!"

They burst through the edge of the forest. In the moonlight, it became evident how old and weak Percy looked, despite his massive and once-powerful frame. The old man huffed and wheezed as he did his best to keep up.

Halfway from the forest to the house they were met by a fresh batch of the evil creatures.

"Nooooooo!" Percy yelled.

"We're surrounded," the well-dressed man said.

"There must be three dozen or more," screeched the hairnetted woman. Now she *was* shaking, but not from the cold creek water.

She was shaking from fear.

The well-dressed man pulled a Taser out of his jacket pocket as fast as he could, but his enemy moved swiftly.

"Waaaaaahhhhh!" Percy yelled. He swatted at them weakly, but soon they were upon him.

They scrambled all over him, dozens upon dozens, slurping and chewing. He fell to the ground, lost under the swarm.

"Noooooo!" the well-dressed man yelled, zapping as many of the hard shells as he could with his Taser.

The hairnetted woman ripped off her hairnet, stretched it out, and captured one creature at a time. She tied them up in her net so the well-dressed man could more easily kill them.

But there were just too many.

Before they could destroy even half a dozen of the disgusting beasties, the swarm left as quickly as it had come. They scurried off of Percy, leaving a trail of monster juice. He had been drained. Percy didn't have much time left.

"Percy!" the well-dressed man yelled. "Hang in there, old man."

The well-dressed man and the once-hairnetted woman worked together to lift Percy's massive body off the ground and drag him as fast as they could toward the house in the distance.

"Gwwwwaaaaa!" Percy moaned through a mouth filled with black slime.

"Shhhhh," said the once-hairnetted woman. "You're going to be okay."

But they both knew that Percy wouldn't be okay. They just needed him to hang on long enough to answer the question that burned through their minds.

After an exhausting effort, they were able to make it to the window at the back of the house.

"This is Chris," the once-hairnetted woman said to Percy.

They turned Percy's head so he could get a better look. His eye was starting to lose its glimmer. He was fading fast.

They could see a young boy on his bed, counting a large pile of money. He seemed upset by the amount, counting it over and over again. He pulled over a laptop, opened it up, and tapped away at the keys.

"Is this the one, Percy?" the well-dressed man asked.

"Guuuuhhhhh . . ." Percy groaned.

"Percy!" the once-hairnetted woman hissed in his ear. "Percy, you must tell us! Please!"

Even though he hated to, the well-dressed man slapped Percy across the face as hard as he could.

He got the reaction he was looking for.

"Yesssss!" Percy's voice gurgled up through his broken body. "Chris. Is. The."

His body spasmed, and as he slipped to the ground, his last word was:

"One."

Tears escaped the well-dressed man's eyes for Percy. He feared for the rest of his residents as well.

"Now we need this young boy more than ever," he said, "but how can we draw him to us?"

"I have an idea," the once-hairnetted woman said, and she held up her hairnet, which contained one of the vile beasts, still alive. It hissed and screeched.

"Perhaps this evil little theeng can help...."

1 Summer x
1 Zillion Lawns
= 0

Chris.Taylor.02: My dreams are destroyed.

S'whts da prb? :**karate247**

Chris.Taylor.02: Shane, please use vowels!

Thts yr prb? I dstryd yr drms w/ n vwls? :**karate247**

Chris.Taylor.02: No, you didn't destroy my dreams.
But use your vowels.

:**karate247**
Thanks, teacher. SO WHAT'S YOUR PROBLEM?

Chris.Taylor.02: Do you remember that amazing
telescope I wanted to buy?

Y! Did u get it?!? :**karate247**

Chris.Taylor.02: NOOOOOOO! I don't have enough money! What am I going to do?

Mow more lawns? :**karate247**

Chris.Taylor.02: It's almost fall! I have 2 more lawns and that's IT! I'm never going to get that telescope.

I'll ttly loan u csh. How much? $25? $30? :**karate247**

Chris.Taylor.02: $484.99 more.

I give u 99 cnt. :**karate247**

Chris.Taylor.02: Ha ha ha.

K, $4.99. I evn round it up $5. :**karate247**

Chris.Taylor.02: I still need 480 bucks.

$479.99. Huge difference. :**karate247**

Chris.Taylor.02: Whatever. I can't believe school is Monday. ARRGGHHH!

:**karate247**
Since when do you hate schl? That's my thng. You luv schl.

Chris.Taylor.02: I don't love school. I love STUDYING.

Same thng. :**karate247**

Chris.Taylor.02: No, it's not. If I had it my way, I'd get my mother to homeschool me. When you're smart, the teachers always pick on you. They think I like answering questions.

But u r always right! :**karate247**

Chris.Taylor.02: That doesn't mean I should have to stand up in front of class and give every bully in school a reason to pick on me. All the kids in our school are idiots.

Xcept 4 me? :**karate247**

Chris.Taylor.02: Well . . .

:(:**karate247**

Chris.Taylor.02: Just kidding. You, Ben, and Gordon are the exceptions. OF COURSE.

:**karate247**
Tnx. OK, now I shall reward your good behavior with vowels and amazing advice.

Chris.Taylor.02: Bring it on.

:**karate247**
Become Middle School Honor Society President! U'll rake in the dough!

9

Chris.Taylor.02: What?

They pay the prez, don't they? **:karate247**

Chris.Taylor.02: Last time I checked, no. Plus, I already declined an invitation to the Honor Society. I can't handle that kind of pressure.

:karate247

Go back and say yes! Don't they have fund-raisers? Fund-raise for yourself!

Chris.Taylor.02: I'll keep that in mind. I should go. I've got to spend the rest of my summer cleaning my bedroom. Maybe I can get Mom to give me 10 bucks.

:karate247

Demand 15! I'll think of more amazing ideas, although that last one was pretty good. LTR.

The pile of money on my bed made me as depressed as the collection of dirty, funky piles in my room. I slammed my laptop shut.

My eye went from the pile of laundry with my "Mars or Bust" T-shirt on top, to a pile of comic books, to a pile of old horror movie DVDs and video games. In one disgusting corner of my room, a comb sat on top of a moldy piece of pizza. Pieces of my short blond hair mixed with goopy pizza grease.

What did I have to show for an entire summer of lawn mowing? Grass-covered legs that itched like crazy, a messy room, and an empty space by the window where my dream telescope should have been.

Hanging next to my Star Wars poster was a picture of the Super Infinity Space Gazer—positioned so that it pointed at the Death Star. The state-of-the-art TRQ92 Super Infinity Space Gazer would show me the craters of the moon! It would show me stars in distant galaxies! It would be my first step toward becoming an astrophysicist—my life's dream!

I scooped up all of my money and shoved it back into the shoe box. Crouching down low, I started to slide it under my bed, when a sound made me stop.

A very quiet crunching sound.

Reluctantly, I turned toward the pizza. Sitting in the middle of the old slice, a large black cockroach enjoyed snack time.

It had just polished off a scabby pepperoni, and was starting to munch on my hair!

"Ugh!" I grunted in disgust.

Grabbing a stinky tattered shoe, I cautiously crept toward the roach.

It saw me almost right away, let out what sounded like a tiny belch, and ran behind the piles.

I jumped down onto my hands and knees to see it scurry into a small space between the wall and the floor.

Its legs scrambled and scraped. It was so full of pizza I wasn't sure it was going to make it.

Just when I thought I'd have time to grab a can of Raid, it slipped through and was gone.

I picked up the pizza, plucked off the comb, and tossed both in the garbage.

By the time I finished cleaning my room, summer vacation was over.

The First Day

When Shane and I arrived at school the next day, it was like we had never left for summer break—a feeling worse than anything in the world.

"Ah, the smell of cafeteria mashed potatoes," Shane said as he inhaled deeply.

He texted me the night before that he planned on wearing his karate uniform "2 mk a statmnt." I'm glad he changed his mind. He showed up in a ratty T-shirt and a stinky old pair of jeans instead. It made my black pants and green collared shirt look like formal wear.

"I'll catch you later," Shane said as he gave me a quick thumbs-up and headed down another hall toward his locker. I gave him a weak thumbs-up back and kept walking.

As I walked, I daydreamed about pointing the

TRQ92 at the moon on a clear night. This helped me ignore all the idiots that surrounded me as I made my way toward my locker. I was so deep in thought that I didn't even notice the huge figure towering in front of me until it was too late.

"What the—?!" I whooped as I bounced off the massive kid and hit the ground.

I lifted up my head to see a pair of sneakers on the most monstrous feet in middle school.

"Chris!" a voice boomed.

I looked up, terrified. . . .

"We didn't mean to run into you like that. We thought for sure you'd see us!"

A beefy, tanned arm reached down to help me up.

"Gordon!" I said, happy to see my friend. "Hey, man. What did they feed you at summer camp? You're like a wrestler."

Gordon chuckled as he said, "Lots of lean meats. Protein shakes. A whole horse. You know, stuff like that."

Gordon pulled me up and I could see another friend, Ben, was with Gordon.

"What were you thinking about?" Ben asked.

"I was thinking of the moon," I said.

"Huh?" Gordon said.

"Never mind; I'll explain later."

"Okay," said Ben, a much smaller dude, with pale skin and messy reddish blond hair. "How do I look? I got a brand new suit for the first day of school!"

I didn't know what to say. His blue suit and red tie seemed really nice, I guess, but he still looked as ratty as Shane did in his jeans and T-shirt. Plus, Ben always looked like he was about to hurl.

"Um," I said slowly. "Ah . . . the SUIT looks great, man!" At least that wasn't a lie.

I turned to Gordon in his new jeans and a T-shirt two sizes too small. "Isn't that shirt a little tight?" I asked.

"Naw, dude," Gordon said. "I gotta make sure the ladies can see how much I trained this summer. Check out these GUNS!"

Gordon flexed, and I thought I could hear a bit of T-shirt rip. He turned to show his muscles to the kids walking up and down the hallway. A few giggly girls stopped and pointed. Gordon flexed again, harder this time.

RIIIIIIIIIIIIIIIIIIIP!

His shirt split up both sides, revealing his slightly hairy armpit. The warning bell rang, and there was a sudden rush in the hallway. No one wanted to be late to the first class of the year.

Gordon's face went from surprised to horrified. "Aw, man. What the heck am I gonna do?" he practically whined.

Ben and I started laughing like hyenas. His muscles didn't look so big anymore.

Ben, between laughs, said, "Come on over to my locker. I have an extra T-shirt. It might be a bit tight. Just promise not to flex in it!"

That made Ben and I laugh even harder. At least my friends had made me forget about the telescope situation.

"Man, this line is huge," Ben said as we waited for hot lunch.

"What's your rush?" I asked. "The food probably hasn't gotten any better. Everyone's just forgotten how bad it is."

"What's the special today?" Ben asked. "Icky Nuggets? Salisbury Snake?"

I looked to see what the lunch lady was scooping out. She was so short that even when I craned my neck, all I could see was the top of her hairnet. But I could see the food through the glass. She dug deep into a pan with her skinny, hairy arm and out came—

"Chicken Not-Your-Mom's," I said.

"It's chicken parmesan, but it's definitely not your mom's!" Ben and I chirped in unison.

We laughed our way to the lunch lady, who stared us down as we got closer to her station. She furrowed her wrinkly brow, but didn't say anything as she plopped a rubbery and cheesy piece of chicken onto Ben's plate. I decided to get the Blandburger with Cheese.

The lunch lady fussed behind the counter for a bit and then handed me my burger with a wink.

We made our way through the tables and found Shane and Gordon.

As we sat down, Shane said, "Welcome back, gentlemen!"

"It's almost like the summer never happened," I said. "Thanks for grabbing the regular seats."

"I think I can feel an imprint of my butt," Ben said as he wiggled his rear on the bench. "Feels good."

I grabbed my Blandburger and took a huge bite.

There was a loud crunch and something squirted out of my burger . . . right onto Gordon!

"Dude!!!" he yelled. A yellowish wad of goo slimed its way down his shirt.

"Is that some kind of sauce?" Shane asked as he poked at his dry burger. "I didn't get any sauce."

The burger was totally funky, but I didn't care. I was starving. I took another bite—so what if it was a little crunchy?

"Arrgh, this is the worst day ever!" yelled Gordon as he wiped off the goo. "Two of my shirts are ruined—"

"One of your shirts," interrupted Ben.

"And Coach Grey has gone crazy!"

"Wait," said Shane. "I thought you and Coach Grey were besties."

"Yeah, well not after today," Gordon continued. "I just found out that everyone on a sports team has to 'volunteer in the community' or we're off the team."

"So," Shane asked, "what are you going to do?"

"I guess I'm gonna have to do it. Coach said that even if we didn't care that it was our 'civic duty,' we could do it for money."

"What money?" I asked.

"He said the local Rotary was giving away five hundred dollars to the Rio Vista Middle School student who did the most hours of volunteering for the first half of the school year. But I have to spend time perfecting my technique! ARRGH!"

"Wait. Is it just jocks who can win the Volunteer of the Year award?"

"No, it's the whole school. Which is why there's no way I'd win it!"

My brain buzzed at the idea of winning the money.

"Okay, wait. No, really, last question!" I was so excited I almost burst. "Where do you go to sign up to be a volunteer?"

"Mrs. Gonzales is the volunteer coordinator. Sign-up starts tomorrow. Why do you care?" asked Gordon. "Volunteering isn't your thing. It doesn't involve books or studying or writing papers."

Shane raised a questioning eyebrow.

"Yeah," Ben asked. "What's the deal?"

I stood up for dramatic effect. A few kids looked over from other tables. "I'm going to be Volunteer of the Year. I'm going to win the five hundred dollars. I'm going to buy the telescope of my dreams!"

The Light at the End of the Classroom

BUZZZZZZZZZZZZZZZZZZZZZZZZZZZ....

The alarm clock buzzed and buzzed and buzzed. I set it for extra early the night before so I could get to school before all the other volunteers. The best volunteer assignment—and the TRQ92—would be mine!

My bed was so hot, I felt like a slug. My eyes refused to open. I reached over to the alarm clock to shut it up, and then yawned. And yawned three more times. My eyes felt like they were glued shut. When I finally opened them, I couldn't see anything.

I rolled over to the window at the foot of the bed and threw open the curtains. Barely any light came in—it was almost as dark outside as it was inside. Large black birds circled below huge dark clouds. I opened the window to let some fresh air into my slug cave, and I

20

could smell rain. Thunder boomed somewhere far off.

Blindly, I stumbled over to the light switch and flipped it on. My head felt as hazy and cloudy as the sky. The lights flickered slightly as lightning struck. A boom echoed through town. My head throbbed, and my stomach hurt. I burped a little burp, and I could taste the Blandburger from the day before.

The storm continued to rage on. It was still pitch-black outside when I got to school. My wet shoes squeaked loudly as I walked to Mrs. Gonzales's classroom. Each squeak echoed up and down the empty hallways, and I suddenly felt very alone. Half of the lights weren't on yet. The thunder still rolled outside. I felt like I was walking deep into a ghost town.

When I got to Mrs. Gonzales's classroom, I peeked through the window in her door. The lights were still off and the room was empty. *I'll just wait for her inside*, I thought as I pushed open the door. That's when I saw it: a strange green light coming from Mrs. Gonzales's desk.

There was a flash of lightning, and I swore I saw someone in the back of the room. I twisted my head around the door and searched the shadows. Nothing. As the thunder faded, I couldn't hear anything but the rapid beating of my own heart. My stomach squirmed with fear.

I stepped inside and closed the door.

The mysterious green light glowed stronger with each step I took toward it.

As I reached the desk, I saw that the glow was coming from a letter—

Almost as if the words were written with some kind of glow-in-the-dark ink.

I picked it up. It felt extremely old. I remembered reading a letter that my grandfather had kept from his first job in 1965. It felt exactly like that—thin, from a different time. An older time. It smelled moldy. It looked like it had been written on a typewriter instead of a computer!

I read the letter:

Dearest Students of Rio Vista,

Volunteers are needed to tend to our geriatric patients' every want and need. Many of our residents suffer dementia, necrosis, and many more rare and vexing ailments. Toward that end, discretion is very much necessary, as is a strong stomach.

Volunteers who are able to tend to

these dear, suffering wretches, for as many hours as possible and as soon as possible, will be most welcome!

All interested parties should favor us with their company at our facility on Saturday next at nine o'clock in the morning.

If you find the time and opportunity to visit, we shall be extremely glad to see you.

Yours ever,
The Staff of Raven Hill Retirement Home

As I finished reading the letter, Mrs. Gonzales's door creaked open!

I scooped up the letter, dropped to the floor, and hid under Mrs. Gonzales's desk. There was nowhere else to go.

The lights came on in the room. I held my breath and crouched down extra tight, hoping that I would just disappear.

Footsteps slowly made their way toward the desk. Huge, banging footsteps.

CLOMP. CLOMP. CLOMP.

A monstrous pair of boots, caked with black goo, appeared in front of the desk.

I clutched the letter and thought, *Someone is coming to get me because I saw this freaky old letter!*

Two massive, hairy hands came reaching down toward the desk . . .

. . . and grabbed the trash can!

The janitor tipped the can into a trash bag, and then left the room.

I jumped up and scurried out through the door before Mrs. Gonzales could catch me under her desk.

That day at lunch, I sat at our table munching a nasty, cold Ick Stick with a huge smile on my face. Gordon noticed.

"Thinking about the moon again, space boy?" asked Gordon.

"Yeah," I said, dreamily. I put my hands on my cheeks, looked up at the ceiling, and sighed for comic effect.

"What a difference a day makes," Ben said.

"I got a really sweet volunteer assignment," I said.

"Yeah, where is it?" Shane asked.

"Raven Hill Retirement Home," I said. "I just need to show up Saturday, and I'll be able to volunteer as much as I want."

"Raven Hill?" asked Ben. "I heard Tami Evans went up to Raven Hill and never came back . . ."

"What?" I asked.

Outside the lunchroom someone screamed, and I jumped. I turned my head toward the doors.

"Did you guys hear that?" I asked.

"Hear what?" Shane asked. "That Tami disappeared? I heard she moved."

"No, did you hear—" I started, but Gordon cut me off.

"You're out of your mind, volunteering there!" Gordon said. "Don't you know what old folks in retirement homes are like?"

"Well," I said, "I seem to remember visiting my Nana once when I was five. But, I don't remember much."

"Well, remember this . . ." Gordon leaned into the lunch table. Shane gave him a look that meant *Shut it, dude*, but Gordon wouldn't shut it.

"They smell totally funky. They mumble and moan. Some of them drool and shake. You'll have to do all sorts of crazy things for them, like change their bedpans, wipe drool off of their mouths, even—"

Now Shane cut Gordon off.

"Don't sweat it, dude," said Shane. He glared at Gordon across the table. "Old folks take care of themselves at these places. Well, actually, the nurses take care of them. You've got nothing to worry about!

Just play a couple of games of poker or Mario Kart or whatever it is old people play now and you're IN!"

But it didn't matter what Shane said. All I could think about was what Gordon and Ben had said. And that scream!

Welcome to
Raven Hill

Saturday arrived before I knew it. I felt like I'd been on a roller coaster ever since finding the mysterious letter—and I wanted to throw up. I spent all night thinking about what my friends had said, and I still wondered if someone else was in Mrs. Gonzales's room when I found the letter. But I just *had* to go to Raven Hill. It was the volunteer opportunity of the century.

The drive to Raven Hill felt like a dream. No, worse . . . a nightmare. Unable to focus, I just stared out the window as my mother drove us to the other side of town. Neither of us spoke.

The sign for Raven Hill sat just off the road. It was so overgrown with creeping ivy that we nearly missed it . . . almost as if it didn't want to be found. The car made a sharp left, cutting off a huge tractor-trailer, and we shot up the hill.

The farther we went up the hill, the darker it got. I looked through the windshield to see a thick forest blocking the sun.

The trees leaned down and tried to hit our car as we whizzed past! I looked up through the sunroof, and could see branch after branch just barely missing our car: WHOOSH, WHOOSH, WHOOSH!

"Mom, do you see that?" I asked, pointing. "Maybe you should speed up."

"See what, dear?" she asked.

Clearly, she didn't see anything, which made me feel even more panicked—and crazy!

I looked down the hill through the rear window and saw no road—just forest where the road we had driven on used to be. The forest was moving in from all sides!

When I looked through the windshield again, I could see a small bit of sky ahead. But the closer we got, the smaller the sky got—the forest was closing in on us.

"Mom!" I yelled.

"Honey, I'm getting you there as fast as—"

"Just floor it!" I yelled.

"Okay, okay, fine!" she said, and then . . .

VROOOOOOOM!

We reached the end of the forest at the top of the hill, but not before a branch hit the windshield! For the split second before we came out into the sunlight, it looked as though the branch had left a slimy green glow, just like on the letter from Raven Hill.

I looked over at my mother, who was yawning.

She hadn't seen anything.

The blacktop turned into a dirt road. To our left, a huge mansion loomed over the top of a hill. It was at the end of a massive lawn that looked like it hadn't been mowed since the place was built.

My mother pulled the car into the large circular driveway and stopped in front of the mansion.

"Have a nice time," she said with another yawn. "Chrissy, I'm so proud that you're doing this."

I really wished my mother would stop calling me Chrissy.

"Thanks, Mom," I said, jumping out of the car.

As the sound of the car faded, I felt more alone than I ever had in my life. Raven Hill Retirement Home looked like it should be condemned. Many of the windows were covered so you couldn't see in, pieces of the roof were missing, the paint was peeling, and most of the visible windows looked as if they had been smashed in. As I moved closer to the building, the air got cooler and had a musty, old smell, like my grandfather's leather shoes.

But that wasn't the worst part. Circling above the home were five or six of the biggest ravens I'd ever seen.

"I guess that's why they call this Raven Hill," I said aloud to myself.

One raven broke off from the others and landed on the very tip of a spire that shot out from the top of the mansion. It stared down at me with its beady black eyes.

It was quiet up on top of the hill. Too quiet.

If this were a horror movie, everyone would scream "DON'T GO IN!" Good thing horror movies are fake, right?

I clutched my volunteer form nervously. An old dude from the Rotary gave it to me with very specific instructions on how to fill it out. The most important instruction: Don't lose it! It's the only official way to track hours for the award.

The old, musty smell got stronger as I walked up the rickety stairs to the front entrance. The creaking of the wood was outrageously loud. It sounded like the whole building was going to collapse. I was sure the place had been shut down . . . probably by the health department. The creaking became louder, but I could hear something else. I stopped suddenly—the air was filled with the sound of hissing.

I turned around and that's when I saw it. The overgrown lawn . . . it was MOVING.

Something was moving through the grass.

Something big.

And it was making a loud, slurpy, hissing noise. Almost like a moan.

Before I could figure out what it was coming from, one of the ravens screamed a sharp CAW and swooped in where the grass was jiggling and shaking. Then there was a terrible scream. I couldn't tell if it was from the raven or whatever the raven was attacking, but it sounded human.

The raven flapped around in the grass. It was straining, as if something was holding it down. Soon, it was able to gain enough speed to burst out of the ground covering. It was clutching a huge brown bug—almost the size of a cat—and the bug's legs were flailing around. The screaming started again, this time not muffled by the grass. I still wasn't sure if it was the raven, but it had to be. I'd never heard of a screaming bug before.

The raven soared higher and higher and let the bug go. The bug hit the ground with a squelchy squish and the screaming stopped. All of the ravens suddenly swooped in and disappeared into the grass where the bug had dropped.

Just as I was craning my neck to get a better look, I felt a strong hand on my shoulder. I screamed.

They're All
Ravin'
at Raven!

I whipped my head back around. Standing in front of the open door was a huge man in a nurse's uniform. His giant round and swollen head was topped with a white hat that looked two sizes too small. He spun me around with his massive hands and then gestured through the open door. He had a look of panic on his red face.

"Inside. Safer. Now."

There was no way this nut job worked at the retirement home. The nurse's uniform wasn't going to fool anybody. I bet Raven Hill *had* closed and this escaped mental patient had moved in. My instinct was to run back down the side of the hill. Of course, massive bugs waited at the bottom of the steps, so perhaps inside was better.

"NOW!" he said again, and used a beefy arm to push me through the door. He slammed it closed behind us. Above us, a chandelier covered completely in spiderwebs swayed slightly as the Nurse locked what sounded like thirty-four locks and then muttered under his breath. I turned around to see that—for a split second—the back of the door glowed green. The same green as the letter I had stolen.

As the glow faded, the room became pitch-black. I was lost in the cold darkness with nothing but the sound of the Nurse's deep, labored breathing.

Gradually my eyes started to adjust to the darkness. Maybe it was an illusion, but on the inside the home seemed much bigger than it had looked from the outside. But just as run-down.

"Wait here," he mumbled, then turned and left.

As I waited alone in the mildewy, cavernous lobby, I could hear activity—faint voices and the occasional moan of an old person. At least I hoped it was an old person—that would mean that the crazy Nurse wasn't going off to sharpen an ax. I looked around—there were a whole bunch of rooms down on the first floor and a decrepit stairway leading upstairs. I looked down at the rug, which was threadbare and holey. Dusty old paintings of sour-looking people lined the walls.

"This is like an old old-person's home," I whispered to myself.

"Indeed," boomed a voice.

My chest tightened as a figure stepped out from the shadows. I turned to face a scrawny man with a pale, gaunt face. His jet-black hair was perfectly parted and his black eyes gleamed.

"Some of the clientele here are exceptionally old," he added, as he adjusted his amazingly crisp black suit and bloodred tie. "We want to provide them with the appropriate—" he waved his hand around the front hallway and paused for effect "—atmosphere."

As if on cue, an organ started playing from somewhere. It echoed through the house, creeping me out even more. He looked over his shoulder, toward the music, and said, "Ah, brunch will be ready soon."

"Great," I said, nervously. "I'm starvin'!"

"Oh, but you misunderstand me," said the man, with a sly grin. "You won't be eating brunch—you'll be helping to serve it. You are here to volunteer, are you not?"

"Yes!" I blurted out. I had almost forgotten why I was here, and was secretly glad that I wasn't going to be the main course. I presented my volunteer form to the slim man. "I'm ready to help day and night—whatever you need."

He took my time sheet and said, "Very well." He snapped his fingers, and the Nurse reappeared with another, equally large male Nurse. In fact, they looked so much alike that I could mistake them for each other. They were identical, down to the uniform.

"Escort this gentleman to the kitchen, and see to it that he lends a helping hand," said the man. He then turned to me and said, "Please follow the orders you are given to a *T*, and most importantly, please do not stray into any part of this facility without an escort."

With this, he pointed at the gentlemen who were looming over me.

He continued, "If you find you enjoy this kind of work once your time here is done today, please do join us again at six p.m. on Monday. We can set up a regular schedule at that time."

"Okay," I said. I wasn't sure what else to say, so rather than stand there awkwardly, I put out my hand and introduced myself. "I'm Chris. Who are you?"

The man eyed me and paused. It looked like he was trying to figure out how he wanted to answer.

"I'm the Director," he said. He then shook my hand, bowed slightly, and left, as if he had a million things to check in on.

I stood in the hallway taking in the tattered tapestries and listening to the slow, creepy organ music. I had a staring contest with a dusty old painting to the left of the hallway for a few seconds before both of my escorts, in unison, said, "This way."

We walked past the stairs and into the main hallway,

passing several rooms along the way to the kitchen. In one of the rooms, a bunch of old ladies sat around a fire, cackling. A large black pot hung above the flames, and I wondered if they were preparing brunch.

We walked past another room filled with faded and cracked leather chairs, where two very old-looking gentlemen had nodded off to sleep. At their feet were two ragged dogs.

"Hey, poochie," I said as we passed by. One of the dogs lifted his head and stared at me. His head was shaky, but he looked right at me. His eyes seemed eerily human. I felt the hair go up on the back of my neck, and was glad when we passed.

We turned left at the end of the hallway and entered a kitchen. Several more large men, identical to the Nurses but each in a chef's uniform, ran around preparing what I could only guess was brunch. Although I couldn't recognize anything, I took in a deep whiff and immediately coughed. The kitchen smelled terrible. It almost made me miss the school cafeteria. Almost.

The burly man with the largest hat approached and handed me a uniform.

"Put on," he said, and motioned over to a counter, where a number of dishes had been laid out.

I struggled to put the uniform on. It was ten sizes too large, but I could still tell that I was meant to look like a waiter. A man stood at the head of the counter. He motioned at me to come over.

Trying not to trip on my pants, I shuffled over to the massive chef.

"Special dietary needs," he said and pointed to the table in front of him.

I looked down. On the table were three bowls of what only could be described as "red" soup. Maybe it was made out of beets . . . or prunes. That's what old people eat, right? Next to the soup were three plates filled with what looked like gray mashed potatoes or grits. Its smell reminded me of the time I found a dead raccoon under the porch. And finally, two plates of finely chopped raw steak, which really just looked like a chunkier version of the soup.

"Hurry," said the massive chef. "Angry when hungry!"

He shoved a tray with the three bowls of soup into my hand.

"Table three!" he added, and pushed me out into the dining area through two swinging doors.

It was the largest room I'd seen in the mansion so far—it could easily fit fifty or more people. Groups of old folks clustered around ten small round tables that each had a number posted on a simple card. Some shuffled between tables. There were a few chandeliers strung up here and there to make the place look classy, but like the rest of the house, it was pretty tattered and torn. You could feel cold air blowing through the room.

I took a look around for table three. I saw the ladies that had been cackling in front of the fire at one of the tables in the front. I looked way in the back and saw table three near an organist, who was still tapping away at that spooky old music. He had a cape on, and was hunched over the keyboard. I wondered if he ever ate, or if they just made him play all day long.

I slowly made my way to table three, passing by tables two and four. I looked at table four and saw all three old folks staring off into space, just waiting for their food. Nobody was doing much talking.

I got to table three, and found three wrinkly and pale old men sitting there, talking to each other in some sort of foreign language. They eyed me as I sat the cold soup down. One of them licked his lips, but he wasn't looking at the soup bowl. He was looking right at me. I stared back, as if hypnotized, and he flashed a toothy grin. His incisors were rather pointy.

"Enjoy," I said meekly, and then turned around to head back to the kitchen. As I left, I heard a massive SLUUUUUUURP and looked back to see all three bowls empty and all three old gentlemen asleep with drops of red falling from the sides of their mouths. One of the old men snored very loudly. *I guess they eat fast here,* I thought.

Back in the kitchen, the chef handed me the platter of mashed potatoes or grits or whatever, and told me to deliver it to table five. I held my breath—the smell made me want to puke. That table was right near the door, so close that I hadn't noticed it before. There, at the table, sat three people with eyes that stared into nothingness and skin that oozed with open sores. *Shouldn't these people be in a hospital?* I wondered. *They need medicine, not this gray whatever-it-is.*

They swayed in their chairs and gurgled and moaned as I approached. Something smelled terrible— like rotten meat. Worse than the food. I looked around to see where it was coming from. When I brought my head back up, I noticed that one of them was eyeing me. Before I could react, it was too late. He swiped at the tray as I brought it down, hungry and clearly ready to eat. The other two came alive—a bit—once they saw their brunch-mate grab for the gray whatever-it-was. I laid the bowls on the table and got out of there quick. One of the Nurses that had been walking around the great room approached them as I left and yelled, "FORKS, PLEASE!" but I could hear from the squishy slurping sounds and grunts of pleasure that they were probably eating with their hands, as fast as they could. I wasn't going to turn around and look.

This was not what I signed up for—Gordon was right. I was serving food to cranky, smelly old mean people. Where were the sweet nanas or funny grandpas? *Is this what I am going to have to deal with on a daily basis?* I thought. These folks were really monstrous—and the staff was, too!

I walked back into the kitchen and was immediately handed the tray of soupy raw steak by the chef.

"TABLE TEN!" he yelled, as he pushed me back out into the dining room.

I headed over to table ten. Two of the hairiest old men I had ever seen in my life were sitting at the table. I laid the steak soup down on the table and turned to leave. Before I could go, one of the hairy old men looked up at me.

His eyes looked so familiar . . . but why?

I watched as both of the old men eyed the meat slop hungrily and dug in for their first slobbery bite. It was actually quite disgusting to watch, but I couldn't stop.

It was only when Shane texted me that I finally tore my eyes away from the feeding frenzy.

Hwst goin'? texted Shane.

I'm already done for today, I texted back.

I took off my uniform and slipped out of the front door. The tall grass was motionless. I moved past it quickly and then headed down the hill. The ravens watched me as I went.

I was so happy to get out of there, I wasn't sure I ever wanted to come back.

Amuse Me

At lunch on Monday, Ben, Gordon, and Shane wanted to know how my time at Raven Hill went. I told them everything as we ate Salisbury Snake.

I broke it down like this: It was insane and smelly, the residents were angry old farts, and I thought the house was haunted, but on the walk home I somehow convinced myself to keep going there.

I still just really, really wanted that telescope, and if I could survive one day there, I'd be able to again and again and again. Not to mention, I felt kind of bad for the old folks, as weird as they were.

"Hey," Ben said, "Karen said she can get us all free passes to the park this weekend. It's the last weekend!"

The park is what we called Jackson Amusement Park, a run-down collection of rides and games on the south side of town. The best thing about it, other than the awesome food, was the Gravitron, the most barf-inducing ride in the universe. Ben's older sister, Karen, had worked there the past few summers. She could sometimes be a pain, but she always got us free passes— so I guess she was all right, as older sisters go.

"Awesome!" yelled Gordon.

"Totally!" added Shane.

All the guys high-fived one another. All of them but me.

Shane looked at me and shook his head. "Really?" he asked.

"I have to volunteer," I said. "If I miss one shift, I might not win the money."

"It's your loss," Ben added. "I went to the park like ten times over the summer."

"And was there any ride that you didn't barf on?" I asked, hoping to change the subject from me bailing on my friends.

"Well . . ." Ben thought for a moment.

"I bet you even hurled on the Ferris wheel," I said.

"Yes," Ben answered. "I was way at the top, too. It was not a pretty sight."

"Even on the bumper cars?" I asked.

"Um . . . yup! Definitely on the bumper cars. I spewed right as I bumped into a little girl, and it splashed right into her car."

"Oh, that's rough!" I said.

"Well, you're the one who brought it up," Ben said.

"Actually, you're the one who brought it up," I said with a wink. "On every ride at the park."

"Ha-ha-ha," Ben fake-laughed.

Shane looked over at me. "C'mon," he said. "Do you really want to miss seeing this kid blowing chunks all day?"

"I really have to make up the hours," I said, "especially after skipping out early last time."

"Were you even there for an hour?" Gordon asked. "They'll probably laugh at you when you take your time sheet to the Rotary to get certified!"

"What?" I asked

"You have to go to the Rotary every Monday at four with your time sheet—or those hours don't count," Gordon answered.

"Aw, man!" I said. "You've got to be kidding! I left my time sheet at Raven Hill. The Director doesn't want me there until six, but I'll have to go early to get my time sheet, then run to the Rotary, then go back home to grab some food, and *then* get back to Raven Hill. UGH!"

"Whoa, dude," said Shane. "Don't sweat it! You've only put, like an hour in anyway."

"Yeah," said Ben. "You've got three hundred hours to go, knowing you!"

"That hour could be the hour that makes the

difference at the end of the fall!" I said, almost screaming. "I need every hour I can get!"

So, at the end of the day, at the exact moment that the final bell rang, I bolted up the main road from school and took a left up to Raven Hill. I bounded up the old creaky stairs, which shook from my pounding feet, and knocked on the door as hard as I could.

Nobody answered.

I knocked again, even harder this time. My knuckles hurt.

I looked at my digital watch. Thirty seconds went by.

Sixty seconds.

Two minutes.

Where were the Nurses? Where was anybody?

I leaped down the stairs and started to explore around the side of the building, hoping to find a window that I could peek into and get someone's attention.

There wasn't much of a path to follow—everything was overgrown around the old house. I slowly made my way through the waist-high grass, avoiding thorny weeds and bushes. It was dark on the side of the building, but there was one spot in particular that was brighter—a window that was hidden behind a bush. And it sounded like something was going on in the room behind it. There was a buzz of conversation and grunting. I could hear chairs squeaking on the hardwood floor.

The closer I got, the louder the commotion got. I could see through the window, but just barely—the glass was dirty. The one thing I could tell was that almost everyone from the retirement home was in there. The Director and a few Nurses were up front, at some sort of table. They were facing the old folks, who were all sitting down, looking forward. It looked like some sort of meeting.

As I reached up to knock on the window, a dark shadow suddenly rose up and engulfed the whole side of the house. The sound of something massive swooping down toward me filled the air. In a flash, I dropped into the weeds, terrified. Something was after me.

Creepy Meeting

I made my way under the bush, the wall of the Raven Hill Retirement Home behind me, with brush, scrub, and grass in front of me. Whatever it was out there was after me, no doubt about it. I could hear what sounded like claws dragging across the branches of the bush above my head. I suddenly remembered the large bugs in the grass the last time I was here, and I wondered if there was another lurking nearby. Then, as quickly as my attacker had appeared, everything went silent. I peeked my head out to see if it had gone.

Across the yard, I saw a giant black raven flapping away.

Of course, the ravens, I thought. *But why would they be after me?*

I crawled out from behind the bush and stood up.

In the distance, the raven circled around and headed straight back toward me. Then a second one joined in.

"CAW! CAW!" they screeched as they headed toward me.

I stepped back against the wall of the house and waved my hands in the air. "Stop it! Shoo!" I yelled out. "Don't you remember me?"

The lead raven looked me in the eye. We held each other's glare for a moment, and then it turned away. His friend followed his lead.

Between the bugs and the ravens, I really needed to get out of this yard.

I turned back to the house and peered through the window. There was still a crowd. In front of them all, the Director held his hands high, trying to calm the old people, who were starting to froth at the mouth and shake. The two hairy old men actually seemed to be howling.

"People, people, PLEASE!" said the Director. "There's nothing to be afraid of—everything is under control. And I'll tell you WHY if you'd just do me the favor of SILENCING yourselves."

The crowd calmed down. It again became hard to hear, as the Director was now speaking very quietly. I decided that I could wait one more minute to make myself known. This could get good.

"The lebensplasm of our new volunteer is especially

strong. It will go a long way in keeping us powered up."

A rumble of satisfaction rippled through the crowd. Through a smudge-free section of the window, I could see the old man with the sharp teeth lick his lips, as he had when he first saw me. A shiver ran down my spine.

My lebensplasm is going to keep them powered up?! I thought, panicked. *What does that mean? What in the world is lebensplasm?* Suddenly I could not care less about my time sheet.

I was looking at the Director through a particularly dirty piece of window. But through the window, I could see him hold up an old glass jar that was filled with some sort of gooey liquid.

He took a butter knife and dipped it into the jar. He pulled out the knife and spread the goo on a piece of bread.

Several old folks grunted with satisfaction. A few even leaned forward. An old woman in the front row appeared to drool a bit as she leaned in to get a closer look.

The director held the gooey bread up to his lips. All the old folks fell silent. The director took a bite. All of the old folks began to cheer, hoot, and holler. The hairy old men began howling again.

A sudden realization hit me. The goo in the jar was MY LEBENSPLASM!!! How did they get it? I didn't feel any different. That didn't matter though—the creepy old people were going to eat it to keep strong—but there were so many of them, and they all looked so HUNGRY.

What's going to happen when they drain me of my lebensplasm?! Will I die? Will they eat ME?

I didn't realize I was pulling the branch of the bush toward the window as I leaned in. I noticed one of the old folks eyeing the window, trying to figure out why a shaky branch was getting closer and closer to the window. Soon other heads turned.

The Director noticed, and turned toward the window. I could see a strange look on his face as he chewed, even through the dirty window. But I knew he couldn't see me. He turned back to the old folks.

I had to get out of there—FAST. If the old folks knew that I knew they were stealing my lebensplasm, I'd be done for. I slowly recoiled, returning the branch to its original location, making sure that it didn't snap back hard. I worked my way toward the front of the retirement home, hoping that the ravens didn't start cawing again. Once I knew nobody would be able to see me through that window, I ran as fast as I could down the road to the main street.

As I ran, I could feel my heart pounding in the veins of my neck. My volunteer time sheet—the thing that drew me to the retirement home early—was the furthest thing from my mind.

I shuddered to think of what would happen if they

used up my lebensplasm. I was pretty sure that I would die. The director had said it would go "a long way in keeping us powered up." Were they staying alive because of me? Was my lebensplasm some sort of Fountain of Youth for old people? Why was the Director eating it? He looked pretty young! How the heck did they get it out of me, anyway? I had only been there for an hour or two!

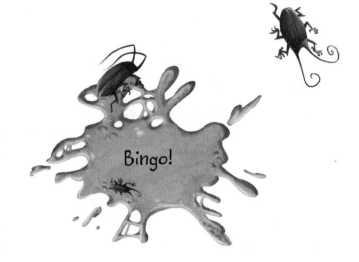

Bingo!

After thinking about it all night, I realized that there was only one way I could save my skin. I had to keep volunteering at Raven Hill and steal my lebensplasm back.

My mother dropped me off right after school. "Have fun, Chrissy," she screeched through the half-open window as she peeled away. Why does she always call me that? I guess I could have told her that Jim Kowalski always called me "Sissy Chrissy" in P.E. class. Maybe then she'd stop doing it.

I stood there in complete silence . . . feeling like a Sissy Chrissy.

Instead of running away, which was my first reaction, I looked down at the little brown bag my mother had given me to cheer me up. She wanted to make sure that I ate a good dinner, and I had already told her that the food at Raven Hill was Grade F. What I didn't tell her was that my lebensplasm was on the menu tonight. *Don't bother to pack a bag, Ma! I'm for dinner!*

I fought against my racing heart and tired mind. They wanted to run. But I knew I had to get into Raven Hill and start investigating. All I had to do was walk up to the front door.

As I moved to take my first step, a single raven darted from the sky and landed directly in front of me. It eyed me suspiciously as I walked toward the steps.

"Caw!" the raven said, and cocked his head to the side. His beady eyes locked directly on me.

There was no doubt in my mind that this was the raven that had dive-bombed me yesterday. And from the look in his eyes, I could tell that *he knew* that I knew something that I shouldn't.

"Fly outta here, dude!" I yelled. No raven was going to stand in my way. I paused for a moment, then opened up the paper bag with my dinner. Tearing off a bit of bread from the sandwich inside, I lifted it up for the raven to see. Its eyes stayed fixed on mine. I threw the piece of bread into the grass to my left.

Immediately, two other ravens appeared and dove into the grass for the chunk of bread. I turned back to the raven on the stairs.

"Caw!" it said and hopped up to the porch. The raven stood directly in front of the door now.

"Okay, I get it," I said. "You don't want me to come in. But I deserve to take back what's mine. Get outta the way!"

"Caw! Caw!" repeated the raven.

Now, I don't know how to speak raven, but the way he cawed that last time really made me feel like he was swearing at me.

I made my way over to a pile of rocks that sat just off the side of the dirt driveway. The raven's eyes followed me. Reaching down, I picked up a few stones about the size of my palm.

I held one up and looked the raven in his beady eyes. "Is this how you wanna do it?" I asked.

The raven looked right back at me and ruffled his feathers a bit. *I dare you,* I could almost hear him say.

I tossed the first rock.

The raven jumped to the right at the last instant, and the rock rapped against the door.

"CAW!" it screeched, but it wouldn't move.

I tossed the second rock.

Again, the raven jumped at the last second possible,

and the rock rapped loudly against the bottom of the door.

Before the raven could even caw again, I threw another rock, then another, then another.

CLUNK, SMACK, CRUNCH! The rocks all hit the large wooden door.

I paused, waiting.

Sure enough, within a few seconds . . .

WHOOOSH!

The door flew open quickly, and the raven was pushed off the front of the porch and rolled down the stairs, a surprised lump of feathers and anger.

I ran as quickly as I could past the ruffled raven, up the stairs and through the door that the Nurse held open.

The Nurse closed the door. "I get Director," he said, and he hurried down the hallway.

Outside the door, I could still hear the ravens squawking—they were really angry.

I turned to look through the grimy strip of glass next to the door, and saw that I had left my dinner outside in the dirt driveway. Four ravens were tearing my lunch bag apart and hungrily gobbling up the contents. Peanut butter and jelly sandwich. Chips. Cookies. One was even working on my juice box.

Oh, well, I said to myself.

Turning around, I saw the Director walking down

the threadbare carpet, past the cobwebby old portraits, and toward me. He once again looked like he was in a great rush to do very important things.

"Mr. Taylor," the Director said with a smile, "what a pleasant surprise. I must say, we were quite disappointed that you hadn't shown up at six p.m. yesterday evening. We were worried you had abandoned the residents."

He stared directly at me, awaiting some sort of reply.

"I . . . uh . . ." I stumbled for something to say. My hands were sweaty. What if he had seen me through the window after all? What if the raven had somehow TOLD HIM?!

"I . . . well . . . ," I continued, "I wasn't feeling very well yesterday, and I—"

"Ah, I see," said the Director. "It happens to all of us from time to time. I'm sure that it won't happen again, will it, Mr. Taylor?"

"No, of course not!" I said, adding, "I'm ready to work really hard here."

"Wonderful," he said. "Well, I think you'll quite enjoy what we have in store for you tonight. It's bingo night at the retirement home, and I think you would do a wonderful job of calling out the numbers."

The director slipped his arm around me like we were old friends and slowly led me deeper into the retirement home. I could hear familiar moaning and grunting sounds.

"There's just one thing, Mr. Taylor," the Director said. "Just one small thing that's nagging me that I really must ask you about."

The Director's grip tightened on my shoulder, and he said, "Nurse Jargon told me you had a bit of a run-in with one of our ravens."

I tensed up. "Yes," I said. "It wouldn't let me in."

"You know," the Director said, "we've taken much pain in training these ravens to guard our facility. They don't often defend us without reason."

As we reached the end of the hallway, the Director stopped walking and looked at me.

"I . . . well . . . I'm not sure what that raven has against me," I said.

"Well, perhaps it's because it knows that you came here yesterday."

"What?" I was flabbergasted. The Director must be able to speak with the ravens after all! "What do you mean?"

"The lead raven," answered the Director, "has his eyes on you."

I stared at the Director with my mouth wide open. I had to say something. Panicked, I reached into the depths of my brain, and came up with . . .

"Well, I didn't know how sick I was yesterday until I got up here," I said. "I'm sorry that I didn't knock on the door and tell one of the Nurses, but I wasn't myself."

The Director looked at me with his intense blue eyes. I felt almost hypnotized by his gaze and his strong cologne. His eyes squinted . . . and then he shook his head quickly. He continued walking us down the hall.

"Very well, then," he said. "I hope you're feeling splendid this evening, but do let me know if you need to leave unexpectedly. I'll need to inform the ravens."

"Of course." I almost choked on the words. I was sure that the Director would now be keeping an eye on me, and that wouldn't help the search for my lebensplasm.

As we neared the end of the hall, the Director pointed me toward the Great Room, where I'd served brunch on Saturday. Now, instead of circular dining-room tables, rows and rows of chairs and tables were set up, and all of the old folks were sitting. I could only see the backs of their heads. Some slouched to the side as if they were asleep—or even worse, dead. Some bobbed around and twitched. There were even ones covered completely in bandages. But all heads were turned toward the front of the room. A large circular steel cage filled with bingo balls sat on a table there. The cage had a handle on it so the balls could be rolled around. The table was in front of the organist, who sat waiting, staring at the Director and me.

"Horace, you may begin," said the Director.

Horace turned around and began to play. Spooky music filled the room. I didn't know what was worse—

that the music for bingo sounded exactly like the music for lunchtime, or that it all just sounded so chilling. I wondered if Horace would take requests.

"Enjoy!" said the Director, and he headed off to other business without another word or glance.

I stood stunned in the doorway of the Great Room.

"Start now?" growled one of the Nurses who was passing out bingo cards and markers to the patients. It was a question, but the way he said it made me realize that the only answer was yes. A few of the old folks moaned and gurgled in anticipation.

"Yes," I squeaked.

Moans of joy filled the hall.

"Come. HURRY," another Nurse said. I looked over to see one of the old men to whom I had fed the red soup gnawing on the Nurse's arm. His hairy, leathery arm didn't seem affected. Apparently, the old folks got really excited for bingo.

The old folks' heads followed me as I wound my way down the side of the room and made my way toward the front. I couldn't stand all of the old, creepy eyes on me, and I felt very, very uncomfortable in my skin. The old man that had been drooling all over the Nurse's arm looked up at me with razor-sharp attention. He might have been a little more excited for my lebensplasm than for the game.

Horace quickened the pace of the music—almost

like an introduction—as I stepped up to the table. I had never been in charge of a game of bingo before, but I got the concept. You roll the balls around, open up the cage, pull a ball out, and call it. Simple, right?

I looked out at the creepy old faces staring intently at me, and I knew that this would not be simple, just like it was not simple to serve food on Saturday. I sighed and looked at the cage. It looked a lot rustier up close, and there were cobwebs all around and in between the metal wiring. *Is everything in this place old?* I thought.

I grabbed the handle and began turning the cage to shuffle the balls. It moved with a terrible SQUUUUEEEEAAAAK. I wondered how long it had been since the last time they had played bingo at Raven Hill. After five seconds or so of terrible squeaking, I stopped the cage, popped open the door, and pulled out the first bingo ball. The crowd of old folks looked at me as if I was just about to reveal the meaning of life. I cleared my throat and said, "B-twelve!"

A few folks in the back growled, "WHAT!?"

"BEEEE-TWELLLLVE!" I yelled back.

One person way in the back still asked, "Huh?!"

"BEEEEEEE-TWWWELLLLLLVVVVE!!!" I yelled louder than I had ever yelled in my life. A gnarled hand rose up from the back of the room and gave me a twisted thumbs-up. This was going to be a long bingo game if I had to repeat every single number three times. I would have to be as loud as possible.

I gave the metal cage another spin. Spiderwebs kept falling out onto the table.

SQUUUUUEEEEAAAAK . . .

"GEEEEEEEE-FIIIIFFFFTYYY-SIIIIIXXXXX!"

SQUUUUUEEEEAAAAK . . .

"ENNNNNNNNN-FFOOOOORRRRTTTYYY!"

SQUUUUUEEEEAAAAK . . .

" E Y Y Y Y Y Y Y Y Y Y Y Y Y Y Y Y Y Y Y E E E E E E - FFOOOUUURRRRTTEEEEEENNN!"

SQUUUUUEEEEAAAAK . . .

I pulled out a ball with no number or letter. Confused, I brought the ball closer to my eyes to see if maybe the letter and number had been rubbed off. That's when I noticed something move inside the ball!

Something black and hairy.

Something with eight spindly legs.

I let out a surprised cry and dropped the ball on the table. A few of the old folks in the front row tried to peer up onto the table to see what it was that I dropped. A few others booed me.

Before I could explain why I threw the ball onto the table, long, hairy legs exploded out of the ball and a slime-covered spider tore its way out. It scuttled to the edge of the table and jumped off into the front row, right toward the head of an old lady with a black shawl draped around her shoulders. She was chatting with the very large man with stitches on his face, and didn't even see the spider as it flew toward her.

"LOOK OUT!" I yelled.

She turned in time for the hairy creepy to land directly on her nose. She looked at it cross-eyed, but didn't seem too worried. She licked her lips in excitement as she snatched the squirming spider off her nose and began to rip its legs off, each one tearing from the body with a *sploock* sound. She put the legs in a small pile and excitedly plopped the spider body in her mouth. She chewed and chewed and chewed, and as she did, she put the legs in a small pouch that hung like a necklace from her neck.

"Thank you, dearie," she said to me with a grin.

Her teeth were covered in spider hair.

I barely had time to say "You're . . . welcome?" before the cage in front of me started shaking violently. I looked in to see that there were more spider eggs. A lot more!

I yelled and stumbled back. A Nurse came over and shoved his big hairy hand into the cage, popping the eggs he found there. Each one sounded like a really ripe cherry tomato being squished. The woman in the front row was nearing tears.

"Don't do that!!!" she wailed.

But the Nurse squished one after another as I stood

there with my mouth wide open in disbelief. He pulled the disgusting shattered eggs out of the cage and tossed them in a trash can next to Horace. The Nurse's hands were caked in hairy brown/green goo, and he looked around for something to he could use to wipe them. Not finding anything, he scraped the goo off on the side of the bingo-ball cage.

My stomach turned as I watched a glob of phlegmy goo drip off of the cage and onto the table. I took a deep breath, only to smell a putrid odor coming from the trash can behind me. I could feel something gurgling inside of me.

As I tried to hold the erupting vomit volcano back, the old folks started to grumble and moan. They were not happy that their game had been ruined. I needed to get the game going again.

I turned the handle, waiting for the familiar squeak, but it never came. I saw that some of the spider egg goop had fallen onto the joint where the ball and the mount met, lubricating the cage. As I turned the cage, the goop became warmer—and smellier. I could taste the puke rising in my throat.

The Nurse must have noticed I was about to spew. He slapped me hard on the back and I swallowed it back down.

The rest of the game went smoothly. I had called out a dozen or so more numbers when the hairier of the two hairy old men yelled, "BINGO!" and then howled excitedly. The howl took me by surprise. He looked so old that I didn't think he would be able to make such a loud noise. It filled the Great Room and shook the windows. Even Horace stopped playing the organ to turn around and see what was going on.

A Nurse headed into the back of the room to grab the old man's bingo card and confirm that he'd actually won. When the Nurse got back there, he scratched his head and looked around. That's when a few of the other old folks pointed up to the front of the room. A mangy dog held a bingo card in his mouth and limped his way toward me.

The dog jumped up on the table and placed the card in front of me, then turned around and trotted shakily to the back of the room. I noticed that he had fur missing in great patches. He was a very, very old dog—the same one I had seen the first day. Where did he come from? Was he the old man's dog?

I looked down at the card, and confirmed that, in fact, the old man had won. I announced this to the crowd, which moaned a collective, "Noooooo . . ." as they realized that they wouldn't win that round. I looked into the back of the room and saw the old man sitting back in his chair again. He waved excitedly as the rest of the crowd hissed at him.

I looked around for the dog, and I couldn't see it anywhere.

Losing Sleep . . . and My Mind

It was only Wednesday of the second week of the new school year, but it felt like I'd been in the sixth grade for two or three decades. Last night's bingo marathon seemed to last forever. The old folks just couldn't get enough. We must have played twenty or thirty games—and once it was over, the Nurses escorted me out the door. I never even got to do any investigating for my lebensplasm.

What worried me were the old folks. The more time I spent with them, the more frightened I became. It wasn't just that they were *like* monsters. I was beginning to believe that they actually *were* monsters. There was no other way to explain what I'd seen! The hairy old man who had won the first game howled and disappeared only to have an old dog appear in his place—

an old dog with very human eyes. *Werewolf?* my tired mind asked. The old woman in the black shawl who had eaten the spider was the same woman I had seen in front of the cauldron on the first day. Was she going to use the spider legs in her leather pouch for a witch's potion of some sort? And what were they planning for my lebensplasm?

Still exhausted from the night before, I shuffled into my first class of the day: Mr. Bradley's Social Studies. You could smell his breath before you even walked into the room. I don't know what was more upsetting, the stench or his huge, swollen, red, bald, spotted head. It looked like some kind overripe fruit that could explode at any minute.

I sat down next to Ben and didn't even say hi. My mind was swimming from the day before. In my mind, I could see the eyes of the dog—they looked so human. The way the old witch—I mean lady—had eaten that spider was supercreepy. I wondered if the monsters—I mean old people—ate my lebensplasm the same way.

Mr. Bradley pulled a small vial out of his jacket pocket and took a sip from it. He did this all the time, thinking that it would calm the breath down. Sometimes it worked, but then the room would be filled with a sickening medicine stench. I'm not sure which smell was worse.

"Hey, Chris," Ben said, wrinkling his nose. "You

look as bad as he smells. Are you okay?"

"They're eating my lebensplasm," I mumbled. The words just rolled out before I even realized what I was saying. The mixture of the exhaustion and stench was making me delirious.

"Did you say 'eating egg salad'?" asked Ben. "What's the matter?"

How could I tell my friend that monsters were eating a gooey extract of me to stay alive? I hardly believed it myself. At this point, I couldn't remember if I actually saw an old dog last night, or if my mind was just playing tricks on me.

"Oh, nothing," I said, recovering quickly and pretending to look awake. "If anything, you're the one who looks sick."

"Ha-ha-ha," Ben fake-laughed. "Yeah, that's sort of my thing, I guess. Which is why I'm sure there's something wrong with you."

Before I could defend myself, Mr. Bradley lumbered out of his chair behind his desk and said, "All right, everyone. It's quiz time!"

"Awww, not a pop quiz!" I yelled it before I could even stop myself.

The entire class stared at me. There were a few moments of unbelievably uncomfortable silence, and then Mr. Bradley spoke again.

"Chris, why are you joking about a pop quiz? This

quiz was assigned, covering chapters two and three. You do remember, don't you?"

I laughed nervously, suddenly realizing that I hadn't even read chapters two and three. "Well, it's still a surprise," I said. "Shocking! Ha!"

Ben gave me a look that said *Shut up*, so I shut up.

Still, I wasn't too worried. I read so much about history and culture online that I was sure to get a C.

At least I would have. If I hadn't fallen asleep halfway through the quiz.

Apparently, I snore. LOUDLY. At least that's what Mr. Bradley and the principal told me.

Ben texted me later that day:

I'm sorry I couldn't wake you up.

Dude, my mom was furious!

I know. I could have shook you more.

You should have shook me HARDER!

Are you calling me a wimp?

Maybe.

Dude, you're the one passing out from volunteering.

It's IMPORTANT lifesaving work!

You don't understand.

I know. Pls, just let me be weird.

    I stared at my sent message in horror. I had just dropped all of the vowels in "please." Things were getting bad. I fell back into bed.

Put on Your Dancin' Shoes!

As a star student, I had a lot of wiggle room with my parents when I screwed up. My mother wanted to ground me for my Social Studies Siesta, but I'd insisted that I go back to Raven Hill. "But the old people *need* me," I'd explained in my most annoying, whiny voice. *If only she knew how much they need me,* I thought. After twenty minutes of begging and pleading, she let me go.

I made my way toward the retirement home. This time no ravens stood between the entrance and me. Pushing my way through the front door, I didn't even pause when the Nurse said, "Wait here."

Nothing was going to stand between me and my lebensplasm.

Beyond the entrance, the hallways were free of any Nurses or residents. I quickly got to the kitchen door and reached out to the doorknob to give it a twist . . .

"Mr. Taylor, may I help you with something?"

The voice made tiny hairs on the back of my neck stand up straight. After changing my grimace into a grin, I turned around to face the Director.

"Oh," I said, sounding completely calm, "I just needed a drink. I'm really thirsty."

The Director looked at me intently for a moment, and then said, just as calmly, "I'm very sorry, but our kitchen is closed for the night. I'd offer you some punch, but I'm afraid it's not the kind of drink meant for . . . a young person such as yourself."

"Punch?" I asked.

"Yes, punch. Tonight, we're throwing a dance for the residents, and the kitchen concocted a punch for the occasion. The Great Room has been transformed into a ballroom. All we need now is the appropriate music."

He motioned me toward the Great Room, and we stepped through the door together.

A huge, empty dance floor took up most of the space. The residents were all slouched in chairs to the side of the dance floor or growling and burping around the bloodred punch bowl. The old man with the sharp teeth avoided the crowd around the bowl by using a long straw to reach it. He slurped loudly from ten feet away.

"Tonight," said the Director, "you'll be playing

music while our residents couple up and dance. You'll find we've set up a DJ station for you where Horace usually sits."

The Director took a bow and exited.

Two old turntables and a crate of dusty old records sat on a table at the front of the ballroom. After I made sure there were no spider eggs in the crate, I shuffled through the monsterly collection, which included The Dave Boo-beck Quartet, Screamin' Jay Hawkins, The Crypt-Kickers, and a bat-shaped record that didn't have a sleeve.

I pulled out the bat-shaped record, but soon realized it wasn't a record. It was a real bat. Its leathery skin was still moist and squishy, and small wads of greasy fur fell off its rotten body. Its little bat face looked terribly squished, but I could still see its sharp fangs.

The bat reeked terribly, and I tossed it behind the organ.

"Sorry, Horace," I mumbled.

I sniffed my hand. It smelled like I had just petted a wet dog that had rolled around in week-old fish and horse dung.

"Ewww." I burped, and my stomach bunched into knots.

I'm turning into Ben, I thought, and held back another spewfest.

The old folks were starting to moan and groan, and

shuffle into the center of the dance floor. They were all well-dressed—but in really old clothes. One old man coughed and moths flew out of his holey suit . . . and his mouth!

To keep them from shuffling right up to me and making any requests (like "May I eat you?"), I grabbed a record out of the crate as quickly as I could, took it out of its sleeve, blew a few tons of dust off one side, sneezed, and then flopped it down on one of the turntables. I searched desperately for a Repeat button so I would have time to find my lebensplasm, but my only choices were Stop and Start.

I chose Start. The record crackled for a little bit, and then a spooky slow swing song started to play. After a short intro, a singer started. He sounded like he was growling.

Oh, I'm so hungry
Yes, so, so hungry for you
Dance on over to my castle
And give me something to chew

A few of the old folks went "Awww" as they recognized the tune, and shuffled into pairs. They danced a slow, slow dance. Their bones creaked.

The name of the album was *Moonlight Serenades* by Count Vlad and the Count Basie Orchestra.

The song was called "Neck Nibble Nocturne."
My skin crawled as the singer continued.

Look up at the moon
My dear
The stars are so bright
My dear
I bend down to you
My dear
And I bite you so right
Don't fear

The singer stopped and a scary-sounding trumpet started to play. My heart rose into my throat. Monsters slow danced with monsters. Banshees. Vampires. Werewolves. Witches. Swamp things. Mummies. Old monsters of all different shapes and sizes.

Two zombies were delicately nibbling each other's necks. The Nurses in the room moved in to break them up.

With the Nurses distracted, I crept out of the Great Room. I went back to the kitchen door, opened it up, and quickly slipped inside.

A Nurse stood at an open refrigerator with a big, satisfied grin. He was chewing on a large, slimy tentacle when he saw me out of the corner of his eye.

"What are you doing?" he growled.

"What are *you* doing?" I replied. "The Director said the kitchen was closed!"

Before I could even peek into the fridge, he rushed over, whipped open the door, grabbed me with both hands, shoved me back out into the hallway, and grunted, "Don't tell the Director!"

With that, he slammed the door shut, and a lock clicked into place.

There was a good chance that my lebensplasm was in the kitchen, but there was no way I could get in there now. I ran halfway down the hall to search other rooms, but stopped when I heard a booing from the Great Room.

The record was skipping!

I had to keep the music going. But I'd be so busy changing records all night, I'd never get a chance to search all of Raven Hill. I wished I could just throw on a playlist.

I rushed past the booing monsters, ripped a handful of records out of the crate, and began pulling them out one by one to find a really long track. Finally, I found a record that had one long track on side A: "Tarantella Transylvanese." I threw it down on the second turntable and pressed Start.

It started up fast, and at first the monsters were unsure of what to do. *Oh no!* I thought, *I chose the wrong song!* The monsters that were slow-dancing slowly shuffled off the dance floor, but luckily a few more came on. The song bounced along with accordions and tambourines, hoots and shouts—it sounded like it was recorded at a Gypsy camp somewhere in Europe, and the Gypsies were partying hard.

Soon most of the monsters were on the dance floor. I jumped off of the platform, and made my way back toward the door.

That's when the old witch that had collected the spider legs the day before grabbed me. Her long fingernails dug into my skin. The rest of the monsters began hooting and hollering as she dragged me to the center of the dance floor.

All the monsters formed a circle with the witch and me in the center. Their bodies flailed about wildly. They licked their lips. Drool dripped onto the dance floor.

I was trapped!

Above the music, I could hear the witch scream, "You're so precious, I could just EAT you!"

She started dancing wildly in front of me and motioned for me to follow along. I was terrified, but what could I do? I started dancing along. I looked around at the other monsters, and they looked energized. Had my lebensplasm allowed them to dance like this?

Monster legs kicked high in the air. An old werewolf howled along to the rhythm of the tambourines. An old banshee screamed with the accordions. The vampires flung their heads back—enjoying every second of the song that had come from their homeland.

The circle was slowly closing in!

Next to the witch, a zombie tried its best to dance. It slapped its knee a few times, and then its leg fell off. It kept hopping on one leg as another zombie bent over and started eating the leg, chomping in time with the music. A few of the other old monsters looked hungrily at the leg, slowed down their dancing, and headed toward the meaty treat. The three Nurses once again moved in to take care of the situation.

Now was my chance.

Great Balls of Fire

I danced my way out of the circle and toward the open door. Nobody noticed—they were either fighting over the leg or dancing like crazy.

I ran down the hallway and ducked into each room as I went. I opened drawers. I looked under furniture. I peeked in fireplaces. The rooms on the bottom floor didn't have much furniture, and there wasn't really anywhere they could have hidden my lebensplasm.

I went upstairs and into the first dark, mold-smelling room. There was a Crock-Pot with some sort of black ooze bubbling in it. All sorts of ingredients were lined up in front of it. EYE OF NEWT read one bottle; WING OF BAT read another. I recognized the contents of the third bottle—the hairy baby spider legs from bingo night. I went through all of the bottles. Not one of them was my lebensplasm.

Heading back into the hall, I heard a rattle of chains and a moan more deep and growly than anything I had heard at Raven Hill.

I froze in place, and slowly turned my head toward the noise, worried about what I would see. All I saw was a door at the end of the dimly lit hallway. It had a simple and clear sign on it.

DO NOT ENTER
Staff Only

I really hoped that my lebensplasm wasn't on the other side, but I knew that I had to check it out. As I made my way down the hall, I could hear the low growl and rattling of chains coming from behind the door. My heart beat faster as I tried to guess what kind of monster could make those sorts of noises.

"Why are you here?" someone behind me asked as a large, meaty hand came down on my shoulder. It took all my concentration to keep from piddling in my pants.

The hand swung me around to face two Nurses standing in the hallway.

"Uh . . . bathroom?" I said, only half lying.

The other Nurse pointed back down the hall toward the stairs with one hand. In the other hand, he held . . .

My lebensplasm!

"Uh, okay," I said as I walked backward.

I stared at the jar in his hand. Even in the darkness of the hallway I could see that it was ONLY HALF FULL! He didn't seem to care that I was looking at the jar—he just kept waving me away.

I turned the corner, but instead of going down the stairs, I hid in the witches' room. I got down low and poked my head out to look back down the hall. The first Nurse approached the Staff Only door. Instead of opening it, he stood to one side and grabbed a candlestick on the wall. With what looked like a great amount of force, even for the monstrous Nurse, he gave it a yank. As the candlestick pulled away, something mechanical started clicking in the wall. The second Nurse handed the first Nurse my lebensplasm, and then walked over to a statue of a screaming demon on the other side of the door. With a grunt, he dug his shoes into the ground and slowly turned the statue to the right. The heavy stone base scraped against the floor. There was a heavy clank and the Do Not Enter door swung open. Both Nurses casually entered, unaffected by the menacing growls coming from the other side. Once they'd lumbered through, the door slammed shut.

I could still hear the "Tarantella Transylvanese" playing downstairs, along with the hoots and hollers of the old monsters. I didn't think I had much longer.

But I risked waiting a little while. After about two minutes, the Nurses came out of the door . . . without my lebensplasm!

Once they vanished down the hall, I crept over to the door and gave it a cautious tug, hoping it would just swing open. But it remained firmly in place.

I reached up to the candlestick, but it was a good foot above my outstretched hand. I took a few steps back, ran forward, jumped up, and grabbed hold of the arm that connected it to the wall. It dropped slightly, but then stayed put. Hanging on with both hands like a crazed spider monkey, I tried bouncing up and down, hoping to shake it into place. No luck. Kicking my feet against the wall, I pulled on the candlestick as hard as I could. The worn soles of my old sneakers slid against the spiderweb-covered wooden wall—I might as well have tried ice-skating up an igloo.

My hands were starting to slip from the sweat. I paused for a moment, held my breath, then kicked my legs against the wall until I got some good traction. Straightening my legs, I felt the candlestick starting to move out and down. Then, with a mechanical click, it released, and my feet slid up the wall. My hands slipped back on the candlestick as I tried to hold on, but it was no use—I was headed for the floor.

Despite the pain of crashing my head into the hard floor, I stumbled over to the statue. Like the candlestick, it wasn't going to move without a fight. I grunted and pushed and grunted some more, but it wouldn't budge. Just when I had given up, I heard more clicking and clanking, like some kind of gear moving in the walls. Maybe I had done it. I ran back in front of the door to see if it would open, but as I stood there, the candlestick snapped back into place.

Looks like I'm going to have to start over.

But the clicking didn't stop—it moved from the walls to the ceiling. When I looked up toward the sound, the ceiling slid open and a giant metal claw shot down right at me. I ducked, but it was too late. I could feel its razor-sharp talons pinch into my back.

"Somebody HELP!" I screamed as the claw began to lift me off the floor. Struggling, I screamed again. I didn't care who heard me—I would rather get caught at this point than find out where this claw was taking me. As I wriggled, I heard a tear and I dropped down a bit. It was my shirt! The talons had hooked my shirt, not me!

As I rose up closer to the ceiling, I heard another click coming from the statue. Looking over, I saw its screaming face turn toward me. *How could this get any worse?* I asked myself, right as a small flame appeared in the statue's mouth.

The flame grew into a mighty fireball. I struggled harder, my shirt tore a little more, but all I could do was flail helplessly in the air. The fiery glow filled the statue's eyes, and, through the shimmering light, it appeared to almost smile as it blasted the giant orange fireball right at me.

I curled up into a ball. I closed my eyes and held my breath, trying to block out the blistering heat that filled the room. For a brief moment, I felt my body consumed by flames . . . then I felt myself falling. Opening my eyes, I could see the floor coming up quickly. For the second time in one day.

Crashing onto the cold floor, I couldn't move for what seemed like an eternity. Finally building up the nerve, I sat up and reached for my back. The whole back of my shirt been burned off—but the fireball just missed me.

I was done fooling around with Raven Hill. The next time I came, I was going to bring backup.

School Makes Me Want to Barf

I knew that I could open the booby-trapped Staff Only door with the help of my friends, but that would mean telling them everything about Raven Hill. And I knew they'd think I'd lost my mind.

When I woke that next day, I felt like a total wreck. My bones creaked, my muscles were sore, and my back felt sunburned. On top of it all, I'd barely slept—and the sleep I did get was filled with nightmares of monsters sticking their long, bloody, nasty tongues into the jar of my lebensplasm, licking it clean. But I *had* to get out of bed and rally my friends.

When I got to school, it took what seemed like an eternity for the lunch bell to ring. I shuffled down the hallways on autopilot: Take books out of locker, go to class, put books back into locker. DO NOT ENTER.

DO NOT ENTER. DO NOT ENTER. I cared about nothing else.

By lunchtime, delirium had set in. Maybe I had just dreamed of the fireball-spewing demon statue.

Nope, my crispy back told me. *That happened.*

I sat staring at my tray and chomped and chomped and chomped, trying hard not to chicken out of telling Shane, Gordon, and Ben about Raven Hill. DO NOT ENTER. DO NOT ENTER. DO NOT ENTER. I swallowed hard and gagged, once again holding back a Technicolor yawn.

Shane stopped talking about his latest paper route adventure, and asked the question on everyone's mind: "Chris, what is wrong with you?"

Shane and Gordon stared at me from across the table. They were waiting for an answer. I looked over at Ben. He just nodded, and I knew that I could trust my friends with my secret.

I cleared my throat. Even though I'd gone over my speech a thousand times the night before, it still felt like the words were stuck in my mouth.

What if they think I'm crazy? I thought.

I took a deep breath and said, "All of the old folks at Raven Hill Retirement Home are actually mmm . . ."

I tripped on the word.

". . . monnnnn . . ."

"Monks?" asked Ben.

"*Monsters*," I finally said.

Gordon chuckled. Ben cocked his head strangely. Shane raised one eyebrow really high.

"So stop working there," said Gordon. "I told you not to work so hard—that volunteer stuff is wack."

"No, wait!" I said. "I don't mean that they're *like* monsters. I mean they ARE monsters."

My friends stared at me with wide eyes.

Shane, whose eyebrow had nearly flown off of his head at this point, opened his mouth and—

"AHHHHHHHHHHHHHHHHH!"

A scream came from the lunch line.

And this time, I wasn't the only one who heard it.

Students ran from the food counters. All the kids sitting at tables got up to get a better look.

"That thing was HUGE," someone yelled as he ran past our table.

My heart began to race. I felt as if telling my friends about Raven Hill had somehow caused the scream.

The Director is trying to get me to shut up, I thought, while looking around for a raven.

"Go on," said Shane.

Trying hard to ignore the commotion and the lump in my throat, I said, "Raven Hill Retirement Home is filled with old monsters. I've seen a few vampires. I've seen one, maybe two werewolves. I've seen, like, four witches. I actually don't know how many of them are zombies. But, they're all in the retirement home together—and I'm not sure why. But what I do know—they're staying alive by eating a jar of my lebensplasm."

"Your what?" asked Ben

"My lebensplasm!" I screamed, angry that nobody knew what I was talking about. *How do I explain it?* "I don't know what it is. My energy? My soul? All I know is they've got it in a jar, and they're eating it, and the jar is half full, and I have no idea what's going to happen when it's empty. I'm terrified that I'm going to die."

Gordon started laughing. He sounded like a hyena. Not that I was surprised. And even though he didn't say anything, I could tell what Gordon was thinking: *Oh, my friend has finally lost his mind this time. Somebody call the loony bin.*

Kids continued to stream past us and out of the lunchroom. Only a few curious kids stayed behind, and all eyes were on the lunch lady. Behind the hot food counter, she was battling something on the floor with the broom. She swung wildly and screamed in Spanish, *"¡No va a escapar!"*

"Wow," said Shane. "Lunch Lady's getting down to business!"

Ben stopped a kid that was running out of the lunchroom.

"What is it?" Ben asked.

"A HUGE cockroach, dude!" exclaimed the kid, and

he made a disgusted face before running off, leaving the four of us as the only kids left in the lunchroom.

"Ooh, a monster cockroach," Gordon said. "Maybe he's come to Rio Vista to eat your *blebenfleben*."

"See!" I said pointing toward the hairnetted head of the lunch lady zooming around behind the counters. "I saw a huge bug like that at Raven Hill that first day. I think it's here for me."

"I was just joking," said Gordon, who started laughing hysterically again.

"This is serious," I said, slamming my fist down on my tray, which made Gordon laugh even harder. "I need your help. I know where they're keeping my lebensplasm—behind a booby-trapped door. If you guys help, we should be able to get it."

Ben looked at me. I could tell he didn't believe me. But he looked like he wanted to so badly.

Shane also looked like he thought I was crazy—but he was just too good a friend to say anything. He clapped Gordon on the back, which stopped his hyena laugh.

"We'll help you get your lebensplasm back. Just tell us what we need to do," Shane announced.

"Yeah," said Ben. "I'm in."

"Fine," said Gordon. "Let's have a crazy adventure! Why not?!"

I gave the guys the scoop on everything. The ravens. The Nurses. The Director. The Great Room. I went over every detail of the Creepy Meeting. I described the layout of the retirement home. I described the monsters I had seen. Most importantly, I told them about DO NOT ENTER and the booby trap that almost fried me like chicken.

If they hadn't thought I was crazy before, they sure did now. I couldn't believe I was talking about things like lebensplasm and monster dance parties in the middle of the school lunchroom! It helped that there was nobody else there but the lunch lady, and she was a little too busy to notice anything at the moment.

Behind the counter, she had finally cornered her prey.

Smack, smack, CRACK.

I swore I heard a grunt come from the floor, and then the lunch lady dropped the broom and grabbed a bucket. She slammed it on the ground, upside down, over her prize. She bent over, and pushed the bucket back into the kitchen with a SCCCCCRRRAAAAPPPE.

She returned to the counter and yelled, "What you waiteeng for? Geet eet while eet's hot."

Students started streaming back into the abandoned lunchroom. If the Director had sent a huge cockroach to shut me up, his plan had failed. I breathed a sigh of relief.

"So," I said. "Let's head up there tonight, and—"

"Whoa, wait a minute," said Gordon. "I've got practice tonight."

"Yeah," said Shane with a shrug. "I've got karate."

"Come on guys," I pleaded. "I'm being serious here! Did you already forget about the Fireball of Death?!"

"It can't wait one more day?" asked Ben. "I have oboe practice tonight. Sorry."

"Fine!" I said, exasperated. "How about tomorrow night? The Director said I could come back Thursday *or* Friday, and I could use a day off anyway."

Shane let out a long hissing sound and scrunched up his face.

"WHAT!" I was yelling now. "What is it now?!"

"Dude!" said Gordon. "You might have forgotten—because you bailed on us—but we've got those killer passes to the park this weekend, and this weekend starts tomorrow night."

"All right," I said, "look. Just come with me to Raven Hill after school tomorrow, and as soon as we're done there we can spend the whole night and the entire weekend enjoying Ben barfing on every ride, over and over and over again."

"Perfect!" said Ben.

"Fine by me," said Shane.

"Whatever," said Gordon.

After lunch, Shane, Gordon, Ben, and I all had Mr. Stewart's chemistry class.

Although I was relieved that my friends hadn't abandoned me at the lunch table, my energy was completely drained after having told them my insane tale.

I stared down at the stained stone-top lab station, nearly falling asleep on my feet. I leaned on Shane—my partner for the day's experiment—for support.

The bell rang for the start of class, and Mr. Stewart was still nowhere to be seen. Shane turned to me to say something when the door on the side of the classroom exploded with a puff of smoke. Everyone gasped, and I must have jumped two feet, imagining a huge cockroach creeping toward me through the haze.

Instead, Mr. Stewart stumbled through with a cough, running into a skeleton set up next to the door. The smoke was superfunky—a mix of burned bacon, burned hair, and burned fart. Some kids started coughing. Others laughed as Mr. Stewart did a bit of a dance with the skeleton to keep it from falling over.

"Whew," Mr. Stewart said. "Guess I should have tested the ventilator system in the lab before I tried that experiment."

Mr. Stewart tried to straighten out his disheveled, slightly scorched mop of hair, but it just wouldn't behave.

My heart continued to bounce around in my chest as Mr. Stewart started his lesson.

"Today," said Mr. Stewart, as he walked behind his lab station, "we are going to learn about the relationship between acids and bases, starting with one of my favorites—butyric acid—which is found in the stomach." He erased a small patch of blackboard that still contained notes from years past, and wrote B-U-T-Y-R-I-C A-C-I-D in huge, crazy block letters.

I heard a small, wet burp escape from the lab station behind me. I couldn't see his face, but I could tell that Ben probably wasn't too excited to learn about stomach acid.

"To start"—Mr. Stewart spoke louder now, comically pointing a crooked finger in the air—"I will ask Chris to come up and assist me."

Mr. Stewart locked eyes with me, and raised his bushy eyebrows. I felt my cheeks turn red. Apparently the teachers had been talking in the break room.

Mr. Stewart was testing me.

"Mr. Stewart," I squeaked, "I'm not really feeling up to it today."

"Yeah, his *fleegerlosen* is a bit low," I heard Gordon mutter from the back of the classroom.

"Come on up!" Mr. Stewart yelled like a game-show host.

I hated going up in front of class even on my best day. And today was not my best day. I was still shaken. My hands were sweaty, and my mouth was dry. I looked at Shane for support. He gave me a feeble thumbs-up and a smile.

The room spun as I headed up to Mr. Stewart's lab. He awaited me with a crooked grin. I turned around behind the lab and could see everyone staring at me.

"Now, Chris," Mr. Stewart began, "can you please open that large flask in front of you and tell me what it smells like?" I pulled the flask toward me and yanked at the stopper. My hands were still sore from pulling on the candlestick. I struggled with the stopper until I let out a little grunt. The class giggled.

Mr. Stewart motioned to me to pass him the flask. "Let me try. It's been in the lab all summer, and the stopper may have melted slightly on to the flask."

I held up my hand and said, "No, I've got it!"

I didn't want to give Mr. Stewart anything but an amazing performance. I didn't want to give him any reason to talk to the other teachers or call me up here again. I twisted and pulled with all my might, and finally the stopper came out, but the flask slipped out of my sweaty hand.

"Oh no!" Mr. Stewart yelled.

Mr. Stewart lunged to grab the flask, but he

couldn't reach it. The entire class watched in horror as it slowly slid to the edge of the lab station, slipped off, and crashed onto the floor. A huge puddle of acid and glass slowly oozed past the first row of lab stations. Students lifted up their feet and stared down with wide eyes. When it didn't explode or start melting student's faces, we all breathed a sigh of relief, only to smell . . .

"Barf!" said a few students at once, and then, "EWWWWWWW!"

The room smelled disgusting. It was the most powerful smell any of us had ever experienced. Overwhelming. Eye-watering. BARFY. Kids in the back started scooting out of their seats while holding their noses.

"WAIT!" Mr. Stewart cried. "It's fine. Remain calm. It's a very weak solution. Try not to think of vomit. Relax and think about Parmesan cheese. That stuff is filled with butyric acid."

Ben, upon hearing that any food was filled with vomit acid, barfed over his lab and onto the stool I had just exited. Shane jumped to avoid the splash.

All the kids ran, leaving a trail of butyric acid and barf down the hallway.

I stood there dumbfounded, until Mr. Stewart tapped me on the shoulder. I turned around slowly, ready for a huge scolding. Instead, I was surprised to see he already had an old army surplus gas mask on. He handed me one as well. "Let's clean this up," he said.

I put on the mask . . .

. . . and promptly puked all over the inside.

I had made it through rotting old monsters and deadly booby traps. It was *school* that finally made me barf.

A Crazy Adventure

We spent all night and the next day trying to figure out how to enter DO NOT ENTER.

Creating a diversion with fireworks in the front yard. Or holding a Jazzercise class. Or having a cooking class with garlic as the main ingredient. Finally, Shane came up with the best, but by far, craziest idea.

Friday afternoon we jumped on our bikes and powered up the road to Raven Hill. As we approached the retirement home, the flapping of our karate uniforms in the wind was the only sound that could be heard. When we arrived, not even the ravens seemed to be around.

The plan was simple. We would pose as elite karate masters and offer to teach all of the residents basic self-defense. The monsters would get worked up, and when the Nurses were distracted, everyone but Shane would slip out and make our way to the Staff Only section of the retirement home.

Elite karate masters we were not. We were three inexperienced dudes with karate uniforms following an elite karate master. And that master was crazy.

We parked our bikes.

"Let's hurry this up so we can get to the park," said Gordon.

"How can you think about that right now?" asked Ben, looking up at the retirement home with wide eyes. It looked like he was starting to believe me.

We walked up to the main entrance. The stairs had creaked terribly when I had gone up alone, but with four of us, the stairs groaned and shimmied. Dust started falling from where the handrails met the porch.

When we heard the creaking turn to cracking, we all rushed up to the porch just before the stairs crumbled into a heap.

"That's a good sign," joked Shane.

I brushed some dust off of his uniform and said, "If that's the worst thing that happens to us today—"

Before I could say any more, the door opened wide, revealing a rather upset–looking Nurse. Well, more upset than normal, anyway. He eyed the pile of wood beneath the porch that used to be the stairs, and grunted.

"I must fix. Ugh!" he cried.

"WOW," said Gordon. "That guy is HUGE. He should be a linebacker."

The Nurse didn't seem to get the compliment.

"INSIDE," he barked.

We didn't wait for him to ask twice.

After closing the door, he lumbered off to get the Director (and probably a hammer and a thousand nails).

"Let me do the talking," I said, looking at Shane. "Once we get into the Great Room, you're in charge. But not until then."

"Got it," said Shane.

Ben and Gordon were inspecting a vase of dead flowers.

"This reminds me of the haunted house they have on the other side of town during Halloween," said Gordon. "Cooooool."

"I dunno, Gordon; this seems pretty real," said Ben.

Ben shuddered as he looked up at the painting of a withered old woman above the vase.

"I think she's looking at me," said Shane.

"Me too," said Ben and Gordon at the same time.

"You'll get used to that," I said.

"Oh, I don't think so, Mr. Taylor," said the Director, as he entered the front of the house. "I've been working here for many decades, and I can assure you that this portrait and I do not get along. I do not like people who stare."

The Director looked up at the painting and we followed his gaze to see that the woman had turned her face away in disgust.

"Wait!" yelled Ben. "Wasn't she looking right at us? Man, this is really creeping me out."

"What is it, Director dude?" asked Gordon. "A huge video screen made to look like a painting? A projector?"

The Director looked at Shane, Ben, and Gordon with an upturned nose.

"Who exactly are you?" he asked.

"These are my friends," I said to the Director. "Shane is a black belt in karate, and I thought it would be good for the old folks to learn some basic moves. You know—to keep them . . . fit."

"I'm not sure that is such a good idea," said the Director.

Shane was dying to say something, but he kept to his word that he'd let me do the talking.

"Why not?" I asked, as innocently as possible. "The residents seemed much happier at the dance than at bingo. I really think they need more exercise. Just because they're old doesn't mean they have to rot."

The Director stared at me. I stared back. The painting stared at Ben again. Ben stared at the carpet.

"All right, then," announced the Director. "I do think the residents would benefit from a little physical activity. I will have them all brought into the Great Room."

"Thank you, Mr. Director," I said. "Shane's a great master."

"I'm sure he is," said the Director, eyeing Shane suspiciously. Shane bowed deeply to the Director.

The Director turned back to me and smiled widely. It took me by surprise, and I stumbled backward.

He said through his clenched, smiling teeth, "Do know, Mr. Taylor, that the ravens aren't the only ones who have their eyes on you around here. We *all* have our eyes on you, and you would be extremely wise to make sure that you don't do *anything* to compromise the security of this facility or its residents."

"But of course," I said, as calmly as I could, and then I bowed deeply to the Director, just like Shane had.

Before I stood up straight, the Director was gone and we were alone in the lobby.

"That guy gives me the creeps," said Ben.

"I dunno," said Gordon. "He's just like any other stupid adult."

"He's not stupid," I said. "He knows we're up to something. Our plan might not even work." I turned to Shane and asked, "What do you think?"

"Let's shake things up and see what happens," he replied and busted a smooth karate move, a big smile on his face.

Shane was always happy to teach people about karate.

The four of us stood at the front of the Great Room. All the tables had been moved to the side, just like at the dance. Word must have spread about what was happening, because all the residents were wearing loose-fitting clothes like sweatpants and T-shirts. The werewolf guy looked even hairier now with his tank top.

All of the old folks shuffled nervously in place, moaning and grunting as usual.

Shane cleared his throat. "Thank you so much for joining us today."

A few weak "You're welcome"s floated up into the room, but for the most part, the moaning continued.

"Today we will learn the ancient art of karate," Shane began.

Gordon walked over to Shane holding a small wooden board with both hands. He held it up to Shane, who came at it with a karate chop.

"Yuhhh!" Shane grunted and broke the board.

A bit of weak applause floated up from the crowd. Shane bowed.

"With months of training and focused discipline, you too could do the same thing," Shane said. "But let's start with the basics."

Shane reached his arms up to either side, and pointed to the left and right.

"Let's work out bad posture by stretching out our shoulders."

Ben, Gordon, and I demonstrated the stretch. The monsters lifted up their arms. Some of them had quite a hard time. Cracking, creaking, and popping filled the room. So did small yelps of pleasure.

"Awoooo, that feels GOOD," howled the werewolf.

Instead of stretching them out to the side, all the zombies held their arms in front of them, as if reaching for brains. Big surprise. A Nurse pulled each of their arms out in the right direction.

"Now, don't be afraid to stretch a little harder," said Shane. "Point your fingers as if you're pointing to something far off in the distance. Look from side to side. Work that tension out."

The monsters all seemed to be enjoying themselves. But suddenly, one of the zombie's moans turned to a screech. He was stretching as hard as he could when his arm flew off his shoulder and toward a witch. The outstretched palm slapped her large witch-butt with a sharp SMACK.

Her screams made the other monsters turn. She stomped at the rude arm as it flapped around on the ground. The zombie shuffled forward to try to save it.

Ben, Gordon, and Shane stared, disgusted, at the scene before them.

"His arm . . ." Ben hiccupped.

"What the . . . ," Shane started to say, but he just swallowed hard and turned white.

Gordon scratched his head.

The old monsters were agitated. Growls rose from the crowd. The Nurses realized that something was going on and looked at one another. They headed into the crowd of agitated monsters to break things up before they got out of hand.

But things had already gotten out of hand.

Just as we hoped they would.

Just as we had planned.

"Now's our chance!" I yelled.

I ran for the door with Ben and Gordon. As planned, Shane stayed behind to keep the lesson going when things quieted.

"All right," yelled Shane. He eyed the crowd nervously, trying to act normal. "When everyone settles down, I will teach you a basic low kick."

But nobody wanted to settle down.

We flew through the door and were about to turn down the hall when another scream made us stop.

This time, Shane was screaming.

We turned to see all of the zombies surrounding Shane!

His eyes bugged out with fear! He held his arms high above the circle of zombies, waving to get our attention, and then fell to the floor.

"Shane!" Gordon yelled, and rushed back through the door.

He was quickly pushed back into the hallway by a Nurse.

"Not safe here!" the Nurse yelled, and then slammed the door in our faces. With a loud CLICK, he locked the door.

Gordon pounded on the door. Ben and I joined him, screaming for the Nurse to let us in.

We pounded until our knuckles were sore.

Blood, Sweat, and Fears

"There's nothing we can do here," I said, frustrated. "Let's get upstairs and find my lebensplasm!"

"But Chris—" Gordon said.

"But WHAT?" I snapped. "The door's locked and we're losing time. Of all of us, he's the best prepared for what's going on in there. He's given us an amazing distraction. Let's use it."

I looked at Ben and Gordon with pleading eyes.

"Okay," Ben said.

"Fine," said Gordon.

We sped down the hallway and my heartbeat quickened.

"I hope we don't see the Director," I said as we made our way into the lobby.

We headed up the crooked staircase.

"I forget—what exactly are we looking for again?" Gordon asked.

We rounded the corner at the top of the stairs and down the long hallway.

"A small jar of gooey stuff," I said. "My stuff."

"His lebensplasm," Ben said.

We stopped in front of the door marked

DO NOT ENTER
Staff Only

"Leg spasm? Wha?" asked Gordon.

"My soul, my life, I dunno. I've already explained twenty times, dude," I said. "But we need to get it and it's in here."

"Look," he said, "I thought you were playing a joke on us this whole time—I wasn't exactly paying attention."

"Did you forget our plan, too?" I asked Gordon.

"No, no, no, I got it!" he roared back.

"We have to hurry," I said. "The Nurses will have things under control soon."

Ben sprang into action. He hopped down on his hands and knees below the candlestick. I stood on his back and got a good hold on the candlestick, then placed my feet on the wall. Ben jumped up and held my feet into place.

"Ready?" I asked Gordon.

"Ready!" said Gordon, who crouched in front of the screaming demon.

I pulled down as hard as I could, and the candlestick popped right out of the wall. The sound of clicking filled the hallway.

"NOW!" I screamed.

Gordon rushed at the statue.

"Huuuuuuuuuhhhhhhh!" he grunted as he pushed. The statue slowly, slowly scraped to the right.

"You've almost got it!" I yelled.

"Help . . . me . . . Ben," Gordon gasped. "I'm . . . pooping out!"

Ben rushed over to Gordon as I hung in place. I could feel the candlestick begin to rise.

"Hurry!" I screeched.

Ben and Gordon grunted and groaned and . . .

CLICK!

"Yeah!" Gordon yelled, and high-fived a nearly-passed-out Ben.

"Wait!" I yelled. "The candlestick is going back into the wall! Pull my legs, pull my legs!"

Gordon and Ben each grabbed a leg, and tugged as hard as they could. The candlestick was still being pulled back in to the wall.

"Harder!" I screamed.

They tugged so hard it felt like my spine was snapping. I didn't care.

The clicking turned to grinding.

"Moooooooore!" I moaned in pain.

The candlestick slowly pulled back out of the wall and the grinding slowed down until . . .

CLICK!

The door flung open. Cold air blew through the doorway. It smelled a little like a hospital—sterile and bleachy.

I let go of the candlestick.

It was pitch-black and eerily quiet inside.

"You first," said Ben. I could hear the fear in his voice.

I felt exactly the same way.

We held our cell phones up as flashlights and headed in. Ben followed close behind me and Gordon. We slowly made our way down the hallway. With every step I took, I expected something to spring out at us.

"Don't they have any lights around here?" Ben asked.

"I dunno," I said.

We flashed our cell phone lights along the wall. There didn't seem to be any switches anywhere. The doors in the hall were all closed, and had small windows in them, like in a prison or a psych ward.

Gordon flashed his light into the first one.

"Dudes, you gotta see this," he said.

"I can't look," said Ben.

I came over to look. It was hard to see through the glass, since a lot of light reflected off of it. But inside was a room without any furniture. It looked like a jungle inside—with trees and vines. It was moist, and the light that did get through appeared foggy.

"What's in there?" I asked, and we looked at one another.

We could see a slight movement in the leaves, but couldn't tell what it was.

"Do you think that your lebensplasm is in there?" asked Ben.

"I hope not," I said. "Let's keep looking."

We headed down the long dark hallway. Gordon and I peered into the next door. This room seemed normal, with a few pieces of furniture and a bed. There was something large on the bed. Something human? Perhaps not—it was hard to tell. We peered in as close as we could.

"What is it?" asked Ben, and he pushed in between us to have a peek.

I was about to turn away when the something jumped up and practically flew over to the window. In an instant, a huge grinning face with razor-sharp teeth—but skin where eyes should be—was in the window. Hot breath fogged the window up, as the creature let out a high-pitched growl-squeak.

We yelled and jumped back, our sneakers squeaking

on the cold linoleum floor.

"Do you think it can get through the window?" Gordon whined.

The blind monster lifted up a gnarled, slimy hand and pointed behind us.

Ben covered his eyes.

Gordon and I turned to see one of the old vampires. It was the vampire that had been licking his lips at me ever since I started at Raven Hill.

"Chris?" Ben whimpered. "Can we go now?"

In the pale light of our cell phones, I could see that the vampire was drooling a little. A wad of drool fell off of the left corner of his mouth and PLOPPED to the floor.

The vampire was hungry.

He backed up toward the main entrance to the hallway. The monster in the prison cell behind us giggled a high, piercing giggle. It didn't sound human.

We were cornered.

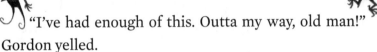

What's for Dinner?

"I've had enough of this. Outta my way, old man!" Gordon yelled.

He stomped toward the doorway and the light beyond. I grabbed Gordon before he got too close to the old vampire.

"That's not just any old man," I said. "He's a vampire."

"What?" Ben said, and finally looked up from his hands.

As if on cue, the old vampire bared his teeth for us to see.

They looked remarkably pearly white and healthy for a vampire of his age. And his incisors looked very, very sharp.

"RUN!" I yelled.

I grabbed Ben and Gordon by the belts of their karate uniforms, and turned down the dark hallway. I had no idea where it led, but I knew it led away from the vampire. That was good enough for me.

We ran past another half dozen doors and the medical/hospital/bleach smell got even stronger. At the end of the hallway, there was a small room with beakers and vials—a laboratory. We ducked inside.

"Look for a door on the other side!" I screamed.

"He's halfway down the hall," Gordon yelled.

Gordon sounded terrified.

Ben slammed the door shut, but there was no lock. We scrambled around the room, looking for a door to anywhere but here. But there was no door, and there was no window. The old vampire would be here any second, and he looked ready to feast.

I looked around for wood to make into a stake, but there was nothing but steel and stone in the laboratory.

"How are we going to defend ourselves?" I asked.

"I dunno," said Gordon. "How about this?"

He held up a beaker labeled ACID.

"It's worth a try," Ben said.

I rummaged through a drawer of rusty old medical tools and found a scalpel.

The door slowly creaked open, and the sound of laughter filled the laboratory. The old vampire was *giggling*.

"Ready for dinner?" asked Gordon as he stepped forward.

He flung the vial of acid at the vampire. It broke and the vampire started smoking, but it didn't slow him down. He giggled even more and lunged forward. Gordon backed right into a cabinet, and the vampire pounced and held on tight.

"GORDON!" Ben screeched.

"Get him off me!!" yelled Gordon.

I jumped forward and stabbed the old vampire in the throat.

The scalpel just stuck there as the old vampire leaned in to bite Gordon. He didn't even seem to feel it.

"Chris! Ben!" Gordon yelled. "Help me out! DO SOMETHING!!!"

But it was too late. The vampire opened wide and let out one more drooly, excited giggle.

And then, right before I closed my eyes—

FWACK! CRACK!

The old vampire's dentures fell out of his mouth, bounced off of Gordon's neck, and rattled to a drooly stop on the linoleum floor of the laboratory.

The old vampire let Gordon go and slowly leaned down to scoop up his dentures. Gordon ran out into the hall. I leaned down to grab the dentures before the vampire did.

Neither of us would get the dentures, though.

They started clicking . . .

And took off down the hallway!

"Gordon!" I yelled "WATCH OUT!"

"Don't worry, Mr. Taylor," said a voice that was not Gordon's, "your friend is just fine. Grigore's dentures are just heading back to his coffin."

"The Director?!" I yelled.

Sure enough the Director came through the door, dragging Gordon by his ear.

Grigore started crying as soon as he saw the Director. He rushed over and grabbed a hold of his suit, weeping into his perfectly pressed shirt. The Director let Gordon go and he came over to stand next to Ben and me. Gordon rubbed his ear, which was beet red.

"Mr. Taylor," the Director said, cradling Grigore in his arms, "you have broken into the private wing. You've soiled my laboratory, most likely ruining weeks of research. But, most despicably, you have frightened Grigore."

The old vampire cried louder at the sound of his name.

"I'm extremely disappointed in you. You were the perfect candidate. But I see now that I should never have trusted you. Certainly not today. Most likely from the beginning. I let you in after the raven tried to block you. You've been up to something the whole time you've been volunteering here. What is it?"

"I'VE BEEN UP TO SOMETHING?!" I yelled. "What have you been up to? Sheltering monsters!"

"Well, I don't really think of them as monsters," the Director said, patting Grigore's head. "Just elderly with special needs."

"Very special needs," said Gordon.

"But," the Director continued, "I will agree with you that I've been sheltering them. It is my duty to shelter and protect them. They have nowhere else to turn. And you gentlemen have stuck your noses far too far into our affairs."

An intercom next to the door crackled and a voice said, "Great Room secure." It sounded like one of the Nurses.

"Very well," said the Director. "Meet me at my office."

"Yes, sir."

"Follow me, gentlemen," said the Director, "or I'll lock you in this wing and open up all the doors."

He didn't have to tell us twice.

No Escape

Ben, Gordon, and I all sat in the Director's office with our heads down.

Shane was nowhere to be seen.

"I can't believe this is happening," whispered Ben. "They killed Shane! I think I'm losing my mind."

"It's okay, Ben." I patted him on the back.

I had absolutely no idea if it was okay.

"Where's Shane?" I asked the Director.

The Director paced behind his desk and stared at us. And stared at us. And stared at us. He looked very, very angry. And still he didn't say anything.

Two Nurses guarded the door. The office itself was actually quite warm and inviting—books on the shelves, a small fireplace, a nice view of the hillside. The furnishings were all wood and leather, and there was a rug that looked like it could have actually been manufactured in the last twenty years.

"If this is your idea of a joke . . . ," Gordon started to say to the Director.

But then Shane came into the room—with the zombie who had lost his arm!

Shane gave the arm, which had been reattached, a shake.

"It was great talking with you, too, Billy!" he said as the zombie turned to leave. "If they ever let you out of here, you should check out the dojo I go to. Remember—start slow—ease your body into it."

Shane sat down next to us. We all just stared at him.

"What's up, guys?" he asked casually.

"Wait," Ben said. "You made it! We thought you were done for! This is crazy! Was that really a zombie?"

"The zombies are actually pretty chill dudes," said Shane. "You just have to talk to them on their level, you know what I mean?"

The Director sat down behind his desk, sinking slowly into his chair. He clasped his hands together, but still said nothing.

"So . . . ," Gordon said, "can we go now?"

"No," the Director said, "you cannot go now. Nor can you go . . . ever. I've made up my mind—you can never leave this place. You've seen too much, and . . ."

The Director hesitated for a moment.

". . . and I need your help with the residents."

"Wait!" I yelled. "You can't just keep us here!"

"Actually, I can," the Director said. There was not a hint of joking in his voice.

"What are you going to tell our parents when they come looking for us?" I asked.

"Oh, your parents will never come looking for you," the Director said.

"Don't you dare hurt them," I said.

The Director grinned and said, "I'm not going to hurt your parents. I have some rare monsters—"

Gordon interrupted the Director with a loud snicker.

"Yes, monsters—in the very same wing where I caught you. One of them is a jungle worm that can crawl into the brain of its victim through the nose and eat their memories. We'll introduce a few to your parents, and they'll soon forget they ever had children. We'll do the same to your teachers. To your principal. To your grandparents, if in fact they still exist. Your friends might miss you, but who will believe a kid who talks about imaginary friends? The worms hurt terribly, but your parents won't remember that, either. So I won't, technically, be hurting them."

"That's disgusting," said Ben, and let out a little burp. "Oh, man, someone get me out of here!"

"What an idiotic plan," I said.

I stood up, crossed my arms, and looked right into the Director's eyes. He looked genuinely surprised.

"Excuse me?" he asked.

"That plan would never work," I said. "You'd have to erase too many memories *and* official records. Do you think the whole school district is just going to ignore all the records of missing students? What about our IM screen names?"

There was a moment of silence as the Director and I stared at each other.

"Good point!" whispered Shane.

"Yeah," said Gordon. "This is a bunch of baloney! Where are the cameras, Director Dude? You've certainly got enough actors around. That old vampire bit was a hoot."

Now I turned to Gordon.

"Wake up dude; this is for *real!*" I said.

"For real. . . ." Ben curled up into a ball on his chair.

"You have seen too much," snapped the Director. "You know about the vampires. The werewolves. It's hard *not* to notice the zombies, and I presume you've seen a few of the banshees. We have a swamp thing. And a monster pieced together from the flesh of the dead. We used to have a Cyclops . . ."

The Director looked distracted for a moment and then continued. "The witches are actually quite helpful with potions and spells to calm some of the residents that suffer from dementia. But, they, too are losing their minds.

"So, that's that. You'll be helping us here until the end of your days. Rewrapping mummies, checking the werewolves for ticks, cleaning the vampire's dentures, sewing on lost zombie parts. The list goes on and on. There's a lot to be done.

"However, I will warn you. Don't think these old monsters are harmless. Had Nurse Uwt actually applied denture cream to Grigore's dentures today as he was supposed to, Gordon would not have fared as well in the laboratory. They are very, very hungry, and it is only because we tell them to behave that they do."

I couldn't stand it! The Director acted like he was going to keep the old monsters from harming us, but I already knew what he had planned. Now he had three more sources of lebensplasm!

"You don't want us to help!" I screamed. "You're just going to feed us to all the old folks. They'll all eat our lebensplasm. Where have you put mine?"

The Director looked at me strangely. He opened his mouth to reply, but before he could, it began raining.

Yes, it began raining *inside.* A light drizzle quickly became a steady pitter-pitter-pitter of rain. It wet the documents on the Director's desk. It wet the rug. I felt it soak through my hair and onto my scalp. I touched my hair, and it felt . . . slimy.

We all looked up to see where the rain was coming from.

And then we saw them.

Dozens of them.

There were dozens of the same cat-size roaches I had seen the raven kill that very first day. And this time I could see them clearly. They looked exactly like huge roaches except for one special feature.

They had big-lipped, snaggletoothed human mouths. And they were all drooling.

It was raining drool.

The rain ended and the roaches started to hiss and moan with their twisted, puffy-lipped mouths.

I looked at the Director. He looked even more terrified than I did.

"SUSSUROBLATS!" he screamed. "ALARM!!!"

And that's when all of the roaches screamed and dropped off the ceiling.

Attack!!!

The roaches plopped down one by one, like massive ugly brown drooly raindrops. The Nurses squealed and bolted out through the door into the hallway. The Director followed.

"Let's get outta here!" I yelled.

We ran into the hallway and turned right to get back into the lobby, and the exit beyond.

"Move it, y'all!" yelled Shane.

We ran so fast, the house shook.

We got to the end of the hallway and saw the Director and the two Nurses frozen in front of the door.

"Get out of our way," Gordon yelled.

The Director and the Nurses didn't move an inch. And I could see why.

They were surrounded on all sides by the massive roaches!

We turned back to where we had run from, and saw a few zombies being chased into the lobby with the large roaches at their heels. They looked terrified.

"Sussuroblats," cried the Director. "Sussuroblats!"

"Sussuro . . . what?" asked Ben.

"I guess that's what they're called," I said.

The sussuroblats closed in, forcing the zombies into the same small circle with us and the Director and the two Nurses. The crawled over one another, hissing, screaming, and drooling as they got closer.

"I think I smell their breath," said Shane.

"Ugh, you're right!" I said.

"GRELCH, GROWWWLCH, GRUUUUG!" cried the sussuroblats. They sounded like they were burping and screaming at the same time, and when they weren't screaming, they were gnashing their snaggleteeth together, making wet, snapping sounds.

They were getting closer and closer. Shane took a karate stance. One of the old zombies tripped over another, and fell back into a pile of them. Almost as soon as he hit the floor, they swarmed him, latched on, and began slurping up his juices with their nasty mouths.

"Oh, man!" cried Ben. "We're roach meat!"

The zombie was drained fast. Just as they finished their meal, one of the old witches appeared at the top of the stairs. She had a small vial of potion in her hand.

"Helllooooooo!" she cried, and for a moment, the roaches stared up at her. She flung the vial down into the pile of roaches that were sucking on what was left of the zombie, and they exploded!

The witch disappeared, and a cry of "Go, Go, GOOO!" could be heard from the hallway beyond the top of the stairs. A group of Nurses, clad in SWAT gear, spread out through the retirement home. There were still at least three dozen roaches left after the witch had worked her magic. Half of them headed up the stairs and the other half closed in on us!

The Director reached one hand into his suit, and pulled out a Taser. He zapped a sussuroblat that jumped toward him, and it fell on the floor. One of the Nurses stomped on the bug, and it grunted one last moan as green goo oozed out of it. Its nasty roach legs twitched.

Shane was kicking like crazy, stopping the roaches with big, squelchy hits. He kicked some of them just as they were jumping at him to bite. Teeth were flying out of screeching roach mouths.

The roaches that had gone upstairs scurried into bedrooms. Old monsters poured out of the hallway, trying their best to shuffle away. Many already had roaches stuck on them, slurping away! The monsters flailed about, trying desperately to get them off. Nurses were ripping roaches off old monsters left and right, but more disgusting bugs came out of nowhere to latch on to the moaning monsters.

But the old monsters weren't completely defenseless. A few of them were actually performing the karate chop that Shane had demonstrated before, and a few of the chops actually landed, sending roaches over the banister and down into the lobby.

For all of the Tasing, kicking, chopping, and stomping that was going on, there seemed to be more and more roaches, and our circle was getting smaller.

A half dozen roaches were closing in on Ben, Gordon, Shane, and me. We backed slowly onto the stairs.

"I can't keep this up," yelled Shane as he kicked another roach in its ugly mug. "There are too many."

"I've got an idea!" I said. "Follow me!"

I sprinted up the stairs, dodging downed old monsters and roaches. My friends followed, and we turned down the dark hallway to the Staff Only section of the retirement home.

"Ben!" I yelled. "I need to pull the candlestick out of the wall again. Shane and Gordon, just hold them back for a few seconds."

Ben dropped to the floor. I jumped up to the candlestick, planted my feet on the wall, and pulled just as Ben held my feet in place.

Gordon grabbed a tattered, cobwebby painting from

the wall to help Shane hold back the roaches that had gathered at the end of the hallway.

This had to work, or we'd be roach meat!

Sure enough, the candlestick moved back into the wall and the clicking moved from the wall to the ceiling.

"Squeeze your backs against the door," I said.

The roaches snapped and spat and screamed. One jumped up and took a bite out of the painting. We stared at a dozen more through the hole in the canvas. Another tried to jump through, and Shane karate-chopped it down. Gordon stomped on it for good measure.

The ceiling opened with a *whoosh*, and the metallic claw came swooping down inches in front of our noses.

It scooped up all of the roaches. They screamed even louder, knowing they were trapped. Their drool rained down on the tattered carpet as the claw lifted them higher.

As soon as the claw was above our heads, I yelled, "RUN!"

We sped down the hallway, the light from the growing fireball throwing our shadows on the floor. When we reached the end of the hall, we turned around to see the claw engulfed in flames. The roaches' drooly screams slowly died out and a few of their bodies exploded in the heat. POP. SNAP. SPLOP. The claw disappeared into the ceiling, and we were back in a dark hallway once again.

By the time we got downstairs, most of the roaches had been cleared out. One of the vampires was still passed out on the stairs. The old werewolves had turned into dogs, and were chewing on a few roaches. A Nurse in SWAT gear kicked a roach, which flew over the banister . . .

. . . and right onto me!

And it wasn't dead!!

I screamed as the roach knocked me over. I was amazed at how strong it was. It had pinned me to the floor, its spiny legs scratching all over me. It crawled up my stomach and chest before I could lift my arms up and stop it right before it lunged at my throat.

"Ben! Gordon! Shaaaaane!" I screamed in a panic.

Now I could REALLY smell bad breath. It was inches away from my face as I tried to lift it off of me, to push it far enough away so I could scramble back up.

"GRELCH, SHMELCH, BRALCH!!" the sussuroblat mouth, so human and disgusting, spat and yelled at me.

"SOMEONE HELP!!!" I yelled, as the hideous mouth got closer and closer. I could feel the heat of the roach's breath on my cheek. I turned my head, and the smell of rotten flesh came pouring out of its mouth. I could hear it snapping at my ear, when suddenly—

"Get over here!" yelled Gordon.

He lifted the roach into the air, and turned it toward

the Director. The Director plunged his Taser into the roach's underbelly, and—

Click. Click. Click.

"Drat," said the Director. "The batteries."

The roach squirmed its way loose, right up Gordon's arm and—

CRUNCH

It bit right into Gordon's neck. Gordon screamed a phlegmy scream.

A Nurse tossed the Director a fresh battery pack. He ejected the old pack, smashed in the new one, pulled the roach off Gordon, and slammed it face-first into the floor.

Gordon clutched his neck, but blood bubbled out from between his fingers. It wasn't a lot, but he was unsteady on his feet.

The Director knelt down in front of the roach and jabbed his Taser onto its belly. He zapped and zapped and zapped.

"I. Despise. You. Nasty. CREATURES," he growled.

Zap, zap, zap . . .

POP!

The sussuroblat's head exploded in a shower of hot green guts.

The Director rose up slowly, calmly straightened his rumpled suit, wiped down the Taser with a handkerchief, and placed it back inside his suit pocket.

No Chance for Recovery

The lobby looked like a war zone. The Director was staring through the glass next to the front door. His face was blank with shock. The Nurses looked upset. One looked down at what was left of the dead zombie and then punched the wall angrily. Ben looked like he was going to be sick. Gordon, who was now slumped at the bottom of the stairs, had stopped bleeding, but the area around the bite was starting to turn a shade of green. Shane, who still had a large cockroach leg twitching in his hair, was cleaning guts off his face with a rag one of the Nurses had handed him.

I had to find out from the Director if we should be worried about Gordon's bite. But first, I had a much more pressing question.

"Where is the jar you're always dipping into?" I screamed.

"Why?" the Director, still shocked, said.

"Just give it to me," I said. "You owe me that much."

"Fine," the Director said. "Nurse Inx, go get the jar." The Director waved one of the Nurses off to fetch it.

I turned to Gordon, who was looked like he was going to pass out.

"How are you doing?" I asked.

"Not so good, dude," Gordon said. His voice sounded like he needed to clear his throat of the biggest loogie ever. "I feel really hot. And nauseous."

I helped him over to one of the leather chairs in the lobby and sat him down.

Nurse Inx came back into the lobby holding the jar. He handed it to me, and I could see at once that there was nothing in it. Scared, I unscrewed the top as quickly as I could.

"It's all gone!" I looked at the Director in horror.

"Yes, it would appear that someone put it back in the fridge after finishing it," said the Director without any emotion, adding, "How cruel."

"WHAT?!" I said, completely freaked out. "Where's all of my lebensplasm? It was in the fridge this whole time?!"

"What?" asked the Director, raising an eyebrow.

"Would you expect it to be in the pantry? I prefer my marmalade cold."

"Marmalade?!" I screamed so loud that Nurse Inx jumped. He headed up the stairs to help the old vampire, who had finally woken up.

"Yes," the Director said. "What did you think it was?"

I locked eyes with the Director. I still wasn't sure I could trust him. By the look on his face, I don't think he trusted me, either. But, if it wasn't in the jar, it had to be somewhere. He did say that my lebensplasm was keeping the monsters alive.

"Where is my lebensplasm?" I asked.

There was a pause. The Director stared strangely at me. He cocked his head like a dog would when you whistle at it. Shane, who had finally realized there was a cockroach leg in his hair, tossed it to the side and came to stand next to me, ready for whatever happened next. Ben was tending to Gordon.

"Why . . . your lebensplasm . . . ," started the Director slowly, "is inside you. If it weren't, you would be dead."

"The day after I started volunteering at Raven Hill, you held a meeting with all of the mon—"

"Residents!" insisted the Director.

"You held a meeting with all of the residents," I continued. "In that meeting, you said that my lebensplasm was going to go a long way in keeping them alive. Then you pulled out that jar, spread that goo on a piece of toast, and started eating it like it was the best thing you'd ever tasted."

"I see you were spying about earlier than I thought," said the Director. "Nevertheless, your lebensplasm was not in that jar of marmalade. I just happened to need a snack after such a long day."

"Okay, fine!" I said. "I get that the marmalade isn't my lebensplasm, but what about the comment? You know—that my lebensplasm is helping to keep the residents alive?"

"You believe that the residents are 'monsters,' as you like to call them, yes?" the Director asked.

"Yes," I replied.

The director looked at Shane, who was still standing next to me.

"And you?" he asked.

"Definitely," said Shane.

"You believe in the supernatural, where others do not. It is that belief, that lebensplasm, that keeps my residents . . . well, *alive,* for lack of a better word. So you see, I haven't stolen your lebensplasm and hidden it somewhere—it's always flowing out of you and all around you."

"So, they're just feeding off of positive brain waves," said Shane. "Theta brain waves most likely—what the ancient Asian warriors call *zanshin*."

"What?" I asked, totally confused.

"Exactly!" said the Director.

"But why do you need lebensplasm?" asked Shane. "Y'all are old monsters. What's happening here? The old vampire's dentures fall out. The zombies are falling apart. The werewolves are losing their fur . . ."

"'We all' are not old monsters. The residents are monsters. I am not a monster, nor are my Nurses, otherwise we'd be just as weak as our residents. My residents are under attack. The Nurses and I are doing the best we can to defend them."

"You're under attack from the cockroach thingies?" Shane asked.

"Yes. Those 'thingies' that just attacked us are called sussuroblats, and they've been draining my residents' energies. All of the residents here are vampires, witches, mummies, the living dead, and the undead, yes, but unfortunately, they are all dying. Their monster powers are being drained at an alarming rate by these horrific sussuroblats."

"So . . . these sussuroblats are draining all the *monster juice*," Shane said. "And you're trying to keep them from the supply."

"Precisely," said the Director. "We've put up a charm around the house and the grounds, but it's been working less and less as their monster powers diminish."

"That's the green glow I keep seeing!" I said.

"Indeed," continued the Director. "We have other defenses. The ravens can pick off a random sussuroblat here and there, but when an army, like the one you just saw, attacks us, we're helpless. We're trying to figure out a way to defend ourselves, but until then, we need a constant supply of lebensplasm to keep the residents from slipping away completely."

"That's why you were looking for volunteers from Rio Vista Middle School?" I asked.

"That was one of the reasons, yes. There are many types of lebensplasm, and the positive, belief-filled brain waves children put out is a strong variety. There are other things—food, rituals, gathering energy from sussuroblats that the ravens kill—which help to supply lebensplasm. Aside from the lebensplasm, however, we really do need a good bit of help around here. My Nurses are wonderful for defense, and for controlling out-of-control monsters. They're not so good, however, at giving my residents the 'tender loving care' that they also need."

I could see that the Director was truly concerned for his residents. He looked up the stairway. The Nurses had cleared all the monsters (and monster body parts) out and were starting the process of cleaning. One Nurse wept as he mopped the bloody hardwood floor.

"Bwaaarrrrggghh!" Gordon cried out from his chair.

He sounded like he was drowning in his own spit. Shane, the Director, and I ran over to Ben, who was doing what he could to help. Gordon was drooling and shivering. Snot was pouring down his nose. He was turning green/brown.

"I don't think he's doing very well, guys," Ben said with a look of horror.

"You don't look well, either," said the Director to Ben. "Did you get bit?"

"Nope, this is just how I normally look when participating in a sussuroblat battle," Ben said.

"Ben is always sick," Shane explained.

"I see," said the Director.

"What about Gordon?" I asked. "What's happening to him?"

The Director grabbed Gordon's face and looked him in the eyes. Gordon shook and shivered. The Director didn't seem to mind. He held Gordon's face as green goop poured out of Gordon's nostrils.

"This is the first time I've seen a sussuroblat bite a human, so I'm not sure how long it will take," the Director finally said.

"How long what will take?!" Shane, Ben, and I said together.

"As with vampire bites and werewolf bites, a sussuroblat bite can change a human into a sussuroblat."

"What?!" Ben said.

Shane and I looked stunned. Apparently Gordon heard the director, because he stopped shaking for a moment to start moaning and crying.

"There is very little research on the subject, because the chance a sussuroblat will bite a human is very low," the Director continued. "But, from what I know, most likely Gordon will soon have a cockroach mouth, and will have an uncontrollable urge to eat garbage."

"What can we do to stop it?" I asked.

"There is no chance for recovery," the Director said. "There is nothing that can be done. The only thing that will reverse the effects of the bite is if every last sussuroblat is destroyed, and that is not going to happen anytime soon. I will keep him here at Raven Hill. You'll have to think of some story to tell his parents. I've decided to let you all go—we would have not survived that attack without you—but I must keep Gordon here."

Before we could argue, a Nurse came storming down the hall and into the lobby.

"More!" he said, breathless. "Soon!"

Invasion of the Sussuroblats

The Director ran over to the Nurse for more information.

"How many?" asked the Director.

"All of them," gasped the Nurse, still out of breath.

In the leather chair, Gordon let out another moan. But this time his mouth was closed. It looked like his lips were sealing up!

"When?" asked the Director.

"Not sure," the Nurse said. "Hour? Two?"

"Let's get everyone up into the attic," said the Director.

The Nurse just stood there.

"Quickly!" the Director yelled.

The Nurse gave a small salute and rushed out of the lobby. The Director turned back to us.

"I'm sorry, gentlemen, but it will soon be very dangerous for you to be here. I must insist you leave at once. Gordon is in good hands."

"NO," I said. I couldn't bear the thought of leaving Gordon behind like this.

"What did you say?" asked the Director

"NO," said Shane.

"NO," said Ben. Although, he was so sick, it came out "Nuh."

"We have no time for argument, gentlemen," said the Director, clearly upset. "I need to get the entire retirement home up to the attic and secured, possibly in just one hour."

"We're not leaving Gordon," I said. "Plus, we might be able to help you like we did before."

The Director stared at me, trying to figure out whether to let us stay or kick us out.

Shane spoke up before the Director could give an answer. "You're gonna have to drag us out of here if you want us gone. You got time for that?"

The Director was angry, but he knew he had no choice. "FINE," he said, so loudly that the windows shook. "Go downstairs to the crypt to fetch the vampires. Grigore is scared of you now that he lost his dentures in front of you, so I'm hoping he'll trust you enough to lead the other two up without the Nurses' assistance. We've got too much to deal with on the ground floor and the second floor."

"Thanks, Mr. Director," croaked Ben.

"You may not be thanking me later, when you realize what you've gotten yourself into," said the Director.

The Director walked over to where Gordon was drooling, snatched him up, and threw him over his shoulder like a bag of potatoes. He was really strong for such a scrawny, pale dude. Gordon groaned, and sniffed wads of brown/green snot onto the Director's finely pressed suit. The Director saw us staring at him in disgust as slimy snot just rolled down his back.

"Believe me," he said as he turned around. "I've seen much worse. Gordon will be safe upstairs with the rest of us. GO GET THE VAMPIRES."

And then the Director ran up the stairs, leaving a trail of Gordon's snot behind him.

"All right," I said to the other two. "Let's do this!"

We headed behind the stairs and toward the door to the crypt.

I swung the door open, and we stood there for a moment. Shane and Ben stood to my right, waiting. In front of me were dozens of steps spiraling down into darkness. A funky cool basementy smell blew up the stairs. It was that regular mold smell you get with basements, but mixed with something else. It was the kind of smell I had only smelled at the zoo.

Upstairs, the old monsters howled as the Nurses tried to force them all up to the attic. In the panic, furniture was being destroyed, glass was breaking, and the Nurses were suffering bite wounds. There was chaos above us, and who knew what down below.

I turned to Shane and Ben. Shane gave a nod toward the stairs—he was ready to go. Ben looked scared about the whole situation and stared off into space. Despite the fact that I was scared, too, Gordon was in trouble and we had to move fast. I needed all the help I could get!

"Hey! Ben!" I screamed over the noise. "Ben!"

"Huh!" Ben's face snapped back to life. "Wha?"

"I really need you to help us, man!" I yelled.

Ben tried to pull himself together. "Okay. Yeah, all right, I'm ready for anything. LET'S DO THIS!!!" He didn't look so convinced, but I didn't have much time for any more pep talks. I had no idea how long it would be before the sussuroblat army made its way to Raven Hill, or if Gordon would be a part of it when they got here. We had to move!

We were about five steps down the stairs, and it was already as dark as midnight. We whipped out our cell phones to use them as flashlights.

Down we spiraled, for what seemed like forever. I was starting to get crazy dizzy. The farther down we went, the more it smelled like zoo. And when I say it smelled like zoo, I mean it smelled like the monkey cages hadn't been cleaned for a week, and when they finally decided to clean them, they used year-old hippo water. Already, I could hear Ben gagging behind us. He was starting to slow down and I feared I'd soon have a barf hat on my head.

I turned around and whispered past Shane, "Just keep moving! Put your shirt over your nose!" Shane and I did the same thing.

The air was getting smellier but cooler. The coolness almost made the stench bearable. But the staircase just wouldn't stop. I wondered what would be worse—an eternity of spiraling down a dark staircase wondering when a sussuroblat would bite me with its drooly mouth, or death by vampire. I was starting to think death by vampire might be the better choice.

Finally, we reached the very bottom. A moist layer of dirt and funk had piled up on the floor. I'm pretty sure it was a thousand years of dust. We held up our cell phones to try to see ahead of us, but it was pitch-black. To the right, water was dripping into a puddle. To the left were a number of half broken, half opened coffins. The vampires had apparently gone through a number of beds before picking one with "the right feel."

We all stopped, and even though these guys could barely gum us without their dentures, I was afraid to move forward.

"Grigore?" Shane called out tentatively. "Griiiiigooooore!?"

Ben, meanwhile, looked one tap away from a full-on vomitous explosion thanks to the spiraling stenchfest our bodies had just suffered.

"GRIIIIGORE?! Oh, GRIIIIIIIIGORE?" Shane's voice didn't echo much. The crypt must have been tiny.

"Come on, guys," I said, snapping out of it. "Let's go."

So, we went. Away from the safety of the bottom of the stairs, deeper into the stank, cold, wet crypt. We held our cell phones as high as we could, and after about ten steps, we found what we were looking for.

Shane silently pointed ahead, and I squinted to see Grigore lying halfway out of his coffin. He snored loudly. I could hear snores from the other vampires deeper in the crypt. Clearly we had nothing to be afraid of. It looked like Grigore didn't even have the time to get into his coffin before he passed out after his adventure today. His huge knobby feet stuck out of the end of the coffin, his toes taking in the cool crypt.

"Whoa. That's disgusting!" Shane yelled into the dark. He pointed his light at Grigore's feet.

Grigore's toes were not only crusty with toe jam—several bats hung sleepily off of his feet. Below the bats and the toe-jammy toes was a pile of bat poop almost two feet high. I guessed this was the normal sleeping arrangement in the crypt. And, apparently, what I had taken to be moist dust before was in fact . . .

"GUA—GUAN—GUANO!" Ben blurted out. A small bit of drool left his lips and he gagged. The floor was covered in a millennium's worth of bat dung.

"Oh no!" said Shane, stepping back.

At first I thought Shane was stepping away from Ben to avoid a chunky shower. But Shane was pointing under the coffin, and we saw a flash of wet, drooly mouths as soon as we pointed our cell phones down.

There were three sussuroblats crawling out from under Grigore's bed!

Heading for the now-screaming Shane, they started to hiss and spit.

They rushed forward, but before they could attack . . .

BAAAAAAARRRRRRFFFFFFFFFFF!!!!!

Ben blurted out the vilest volley of vomit ever known to man.

He covered the sussuroblats!

Their hissing turned into sizzling . . .

. . . and they quickly disintegrated before our eyes!

"Barf!" I cried out. "Their weakness is BARF!"

Buckets
of Barf

When we got up to the attic, the Director and Gordon were nowhere to be found. It was pure chaos up there—the old monsters were restless and scared. The Nurses were trying to calm them down, but were ending up with a lot of teeth marks on their beefy arms. I wondered why—with all of the biting—none of the Nurses had turned into vampires, zombies, or werewolves yet.

We handed the three stunned old vampires over to a Nurse, and then took a minute to brainstorm what we were going to tell the Director about Ben's barf.

"We should just get to barfing!" said Shane. "And we should find out if the Nurses and the old monsters could work up some barf as well."

"Do monsters barf?" asked Ben.

"Even if monsters barf, which I'm not sure they do,

we'll never have enough barf!" I yelled. "There's only so much lunch everyone can lose. Not everyone's as good at it as Ben, and his massive spew only killed three of the sussuroblats."

"Good point," said Shane. "How can we get people to barf even more?"

We stood listening to all of the monsters howl, growl, and moan. I tried hard to think of all the barfy things that had happened to me in my life. Suddenly, it hit me.

"WAIT!" I yelled so loud that one of the banshees nearby let out a scream. "Parmesan cheese!"

"What?" Shane asked.

"Oh, right!" Ben said. "How could I forget! The same acid found in barf is also found in Parmesan cheese! Buh . . . byuh . . ."

"Butyric acid!" said Shane.

"YES!" all three of us yelled.

"We just need a whole bunch of Parmesan cheese!" I said.

"But how?" asked Ben. "How are we going to get enough Parmesan cheese? We don't have time to go door-to-door asking for Parmesan-cheese donations. And there's no way we'd be able to buy enough of the stuff. I remember my mother saying that it's superexpensive. I've got, like, five bucks and a few pennies."

"Let's see . . . ," Shane said as he stared off into the distance.

"We'll have to ask the Director for money," I said, and ran over to a Nurse to see where the Director was.

"Busy!" said the Nurse.

"But this is important!" I said. "If I get money from the Director, a few hundred dollars, we might be able to fight the sussuroblats."

"No money at Raven Hill," said the Nurse. "Barter system. Donations."

"What about the kitchen?" I asked. "Do you guys have Parmesan cheese in the pantry?"

"One canister," said the Nurse.

He held one hand five inches above the other to indicate that the canister was quite small.

"That's it?!" I screamed.

"Too expensive," the Nurse said, and then started walking over to check on the elbow of the vampire that had fallen on the stairs earlier.

"Wait!" I yelled. "How long until the next sussuroblats arrive?"

"Sunset," he said.

"How many?" I asked.

"Ninety or a hundred."

As I walked back over to Ben and Shane, I knew what I had to do.

"I'm sorry, man," Shane said, "but we got nothin'."

"That's okay," I said. "We can use the money I was saving for my telescope."

"What?!" both of my friends yelled at the same time.

"It's okay," I said. "Gordon's way more important. If he hadn't saved me, I would be the one turning into a cockroach. Now, we don't have much time. Shane, find out when sunset is. Ben, you and I need to figure out where we're going to find the most Parmesan for our buck."

Fifteen minutes later, Ben, Shane, and I left my house with my five hundred and twenty dollars. Ben had come up with the genius idea to head to the local Italian restaurant, Mama Francesca's, and see how much Parmesan cheese we could get for the amount of money we had. Shane was pulling his younger brother's little red wagon behind him, and we all had our biggest backpacks, in the hope that we could fill everything up with cheese.

"We've got forty-five minutes left until sunset," said Shane.

"All right," I said. "Let's just get as much as we can, and then we'll figure out what to do with it. But start thinking."

I wondered what could be done with the Parmesan, and I just couldn't figure it out. Did we melt it and pour it over the side of the retirement home? Did we feed it to the ravens and have them poop on the roaches? It really did depend on how much we got, and how much time we had when we left the restaurant.

We walked up to Mama Francesca's, which was

packed for dinner. There was a huge line coming out of the front door.

"We should just go in the back," Shane said. "There has to be a door into the kitchen. You know, for deliveries. Deliveries of huge wheels of Parmesan cheese."

We started to walk around back.

"It comes in wheels?" asked Ben.

"I don't care which way it comes," I said, "I just want as much of it as possible."

"Cross your fingers," said Shane. "We could get booted out of the kitchen before we can even ask."

Less than five minutes later, my five hundred and twenty dollars had bought us admission to the walk-in refrigerator. We could walk out with as much Parmesan cheese as we could carry. Mama Francesca herself pointed over to an eight-foot-tall rack that was filled completely with Parmesan. Grated Parmesan. Chunks of Parmesan. Parmesan wheels. Our eyes bugged as we gazed upon what must have been the largest collection of Parmesan cheese in the universe.

"Okay," I said. "Let's get as much as we can and get out of here!"

"Yeah, let's get goin'," said Ben. "It smells a little like . . ."

"BARF!" Shane and I said.

"Yep," said Ben.

"Forty minutes!" yelled Shane.

Eat That,
Roaches!

Fifteen minutes later, Ben, Shane, and I headed up the road to Raven Hill Retirement Home. We were weighed down by our backpacks, which were completely full of cheese. We also had to move slowly so that the mountain of cheese on top of the red wagon didn't crumble and spill over the sides.

"I don't think I can make it," wheezed Ben. "We should have called your mother, Chris!"

"We wouldn't have had time for all the explaining," I huffed.

"Carrying a hundred pounds of Parmesan cheese is a normal rite of passage for any middle-schooler," said Shane. "I'm. Sure. She. Would. Have. Understood."

Shane stopped, breathing heavy.

"Here, let me take the wagon," I said to Shane. "It's my turn."

"Okay," said Ben. "We're almost there! How much time is left, Shane?"

"Twenty-five minutes!" Shane yelled.

"It's going to take us five more minutes to get up the hill. What are we going to do in twenty minutes?" Ben asked.

"Well . . . ," I said.

"What?" asked Shane.

"Wait, I'm thinking!" I yelled back.

We crept up the side of the hill in silence for a minute, while I thought so hard that my brain hurt.

"I think the most important thing to do is to keep the roaches from coming inside the retirement home," I finally said.

"Why?" asked Ben.

"Because once they're inside, they can crawl around wherever they want—through cracks, up walls, even on ceilings. If we can keep them from getting inside, then we'd have a little more time to figure out how to defeat them."

"Well," said Shane, "why don't we just lay down one big circle of cheese, all the way around the retirement home? They'd creep up to the house, but not be able to crawl up to the door or through any windows."

"But we know a few of them came in through the crypt," I said.

"That's fine," said Shane. "We just have to spread some cheese at the bottom of the stairs."

"This just might work!" I yelled.

We got up to the top of the hill, and were greeted with the excited caws of the ravens. I cupped my hands around my mouth and screamed out a message that I knew the ravens would deliver to the Director.

"We're back with Parmesan cheese! If we spread it around the retirement home and in the crypt, we should be able to keep the sussuroblats out. We have chunks of Parmesan cheese for each of the residents to hold for protection!!!"

Sure enough, one of the ravens flew away to deliver the message.

"Twenty minutes!" yelled Shane.

A shiver ran through my spine. Twenty minutes to sunset. The light was fading, and it was getting cold outside. I wondered if this crazy idea would even work. Whoever heard of Parmesan cheese defeating monsters? *Oh, well,* I thought, *Dracula hated garlic and giant cockroaches hate Parmesan cheese. I guess monsters just don't like Italian food. . . .*

There was no time to think, or to be scared.

"All right!" I barked orders. "I've got the backpack of cheese chunks! I'll head into the home and get the

Nurses to distribute them to the residents. You guys start laying a trail of Parmesan cheese around the building. It's got to be deep enough to keep the roaches away, but I'll still need enough to fill up a backpack for the crypt! HURRY!"

I ran into the retirement home and upstairs to the attic. The Director was waiting for me.

"How sure are you that this is going to work?" the Director asked. He looked completely scared—more scared than I was.

Terrified monsters huddled in small groups around the large, open attic. Gordon was nowhere to be found.

"Where's Gordon?" I asked.

"I asked the first question," said the Director.

"WHERE'S GORDON?!" I screamed. Grigore started crying again.

"He's in a private room in the back of the attic, but—"

I didn't even let the Director finish. I walked past him and handed him the bag of Parmesan chunks.

"Pass these out!" I ordered him.

I walked into the back of the attic, looking for a door.

"Mr. Taylor, I really don't think you should see Gordon," said the Director nervously.

I opened the door.

"MR. TAYLOR!" the Director yelled.

I walked inside. Gordon was slouched over in a chair in front of a small table. His back was toward the door, so

I ran up to him and tapped him on the shoulder.

"Gordon?" I asked.

Gordon slowly turned around, and that's when I saw . . .

HIS MOUTH WAS NOW A COCKROACH MOUTH!

He looked up at me and his eyes filled with tears. He tried to talk, but his cockroach mouth just chattered and drooled a brown substance onto his karate uniform and mixed with the green snot stains from before. He smelled terrible.

"Gordon!" I yelled, and jumped back. I couldn't help it. My friend looked absolutely disgusting!

From the door, the Director called for me one more time.

"Mr. Taylor," he said, "I'm dreadfully sorry. The witches tried a few potions, but nothing worked. All we can do is keep him comfortable, and feed him garbage."

At the sound of the word "garbage," Gordon nodded his head enthusiastically and rubbed his stomach.

"I have to secure the crypt," I said. "I'll grab some garbage on my way back up."

Gordon gave me a thumbs-up.

I walked with the Director back out of the room and toward the stairs.

"There should be enough Parmesan chunks in that backpack for every resident and Nurse," I said. "I'll be back."

The Sussuroblats
MUST DIE!

As the sun faded, everyone—monster and human alike—waited in the attic silently to see what would happen next. The residents clutched their chunks of Parmesan cheese as if they were the most precious things in the world. The Director paced continuously back and forth along the creaky attic floorboards. The Nurses tended to the residents that had been wounded in the last attack. Everyone looked upset and scared.

Ben, Gordon, Shane, and I were in Gordon's room. Gordon had just eaten some coffee grinds and a banana peel that I had brought up from the kitchen.

"Good stuff?" asked Shane.

Gordon gave a big thumbs-up and patted his belly.

"We'll need to take you to New York City," said Shane. "I hear that the garbage there is great!"

"We're not going to New York City!" I yelled. "Because we're going to kill those sussuroblats and get Gordon's mouth back!"

"Sorry," said Shane.

Ben had stuck his head out of the window to get some fresh air. He couldn't handle Gordon's smell, and I didn't think he or anyone else from school would hang with him much if the cockroach mouth became permanent. Ben pulled his head back into the room for a minute.

"Is it time?" he asked.

Shane looked at the time on his cell phone.

"One minute until sundown," he said.

Shane and I went over to the window to look out with Ben. It was eerily quiet as usual. I tilted my head up and looked to see the raven's nest at the top of the retirement home. One raven sat in the nest. It was looking to see what happened next, just like we were.

"And . . . sundown!" said Shane.

Off in the distance, the GRELCHing of the sussuroblats could be heard. At first it echoed faintly through the night, but soon it grew louder and louder.

"There!" yelled Shane, and he pointed down the road we had just come up. Sure enough, a handful of large, drooly cockroaches were on their way up the side of the hill.

"And there!" yelled Ben. His head was tilted all the

way to the right, and he was looking around the side of the building.

Butterflies bounced around in my stomach. I knew that this was the moment of truth—the moment we would see if our shield of cheese worked.

"GRELCH, GROOOOLCH, BLULCCHH!"

The sound of the sussuroblats was overwhelming. The grelching began to terrify the old monsters. I could hear stomping feet and squeals of panic through the door to Gordon's room. Gordon started panicking as well. His roach mouth let out little whispers of grelching and grolching.

"They're almost up to the Parmesan cheese that Ben and I laid down," said Shane.

I could see it from the attic window. My friends did a good job of laying the stuff down—too good of a job. All the cheese we had left now was the chunks that the old monsters were holding. The zombies had already eaten theirs.

"Look, one's run up front to check it out," Ben said.

There was a single sussuroblat—a really drooly one—that was now chewing into the protective ring of cheese.

At first, it sounded like he was enjoying it, almost like when they were dining on the zombie in the lobby. Then, its "yum-yum" slurpy sounds turned to screeches of pain. Its lips burst into flames, and it screamed even louder, its drool unable to put out the flames no matter how hard it sputtered.

"YES!" Ben said. "It works!"

"Yeah," yelled Shane at the sussuroblats. "EAT THAT!"

Shane's remark angered the sussuroblats, and they all began to shout and grelch and snap their snaggleteeth even more. They were all close to the ring, but none of them would go over it. They just got angrier and angrier, snapping and screaming and spitting.

"All right!" I said, pulling my head back into the room from the window. "That's Phase One, gentlemen! We've secured the retirement home!"

"Phase One?" asked Ben. "What's Phase Two?"

"We've got to get Gordon's mouth back," I said. "And the only way to do that is to destroy every last sussuroblat."

"Ah, Chris . . ." Shane said. "We might have a problem."

"What is it?" I asked, and looked down.

"Over there . . ." Shane pointed. "It looks like all of the sussuroblats are gathering in one spot, and taking turns to . . . drool."

Dozens of sussuroblats spat huge juicy wads of drool and phlegm onto one section of the Parmesan ring that we had built.

"Their drool is going to wash it away!" I yelled.

I jumped away from the window again, and paced the room nervously.

"We have to think of a way to destroy these things!" I yelled. "I can't believe they're going to make it through the cheese! Maybe we do need to throw up buckets of barf after all. Or figure out another way to get butyric acid. From Mr. Stewart?"

"No," said Ben, "I think you knocked out his supply!"

"All right," I said. "We have to think of a way to create as much barf as possible. Quick, Ben, you're the expert. When you think about bucketloads of barf, what do you think?"

"Uhhh . . ." Ben started. "Cafeteria food. Speaking in front of people. Talking to girls. Eating too much ice cream. Brussels sprouts. The Gravitron . . ."

Suddenly, Ben's face lit up.

"The GRAVITRON!" Ben yelled. "Oh, man, I never barfed more than on the Gravitron! That would be perfect!"

"And we've got weekend passes from Karen," I yelled. "Let's get to the park!"

"I don't think we have time to get over to the Gravitron and back," said Shane. "Plus, I don't think there's any way we can get off of the hill without the sussuroblats noticing."

"No, we *need* the sussuroblats to notice," Ben said. "In fact, we need to lead the sussuroblats there. They're the ones that need to go into the Gravitron. They're the ones that need to barf—all over themselves."

"Oh, man, that's genius," I said. "But how do we get them into the Gravitron? We could use some sort of bait, but . . ."

"But then they'd eat the bait," said Ben.

"Unless the bait could fly away," said Shane.

"What?" Ben and I said at the same time.

Shane took another peek outside of the window.

"It looks like we've got about five, maybe ten minutes at the most before our cheese barrier is broken," said Shane. "So we need to work fast."

Ben and I still had our hands up like *What?* Shane just kept on going.

"Follow me."

A Batty Plan

The old monsters were still panicked in the main section of the attic. They knew their doom was near. The ones that could stand up shuffled over to Shane and me as we met the Director.

"The line of defense?" asked the Director.

"It doesn't look good," I said.

The director nodded to the Nurses, and they started putting on their SWAT gear and unpacking different types of clubs.

"But we've got an idea," said Shane.

"Let's hear it," sighed the Director.

I could tell he thought Raven Hill was finished. A few more of the monsters shuffled over to listen. They still gripped their Parmesan cheese chunks.

"We're going to take the sussuroblats to the

Gravitron at Jackson Amusement Park," I said.

"You're trying to get them to vomit on themselves?" the Director asked.

"Exactly," I said.

"And how do you propose to get them there?" the Director asked.

Shane turned to the Director.

"We need to lure the sussuroblats into the Gravitron," said Shane. "But whoever we use as bait to draw them in would be eaten in seconds. So, we need one of the vampires to be the bait. They can turn into bats and fly away, right?"

Shane looked around to find the vampires. The three old vampires made their way over to us. Two of them held their heads down.

"No," one croaked. "It's too hard. Ve're too old."

The third stepped forward. Grigore.

"Vait," he said.

Grigore had a bizarre look on his face. He gritted his dentures and started concentrating. The veins popped out of his bald head. He grunted. With a POP, two bat wings sprang out of either side of his head. It was really quite ridiculous, but he didn't find it funny—in fact it seemed to startle him. He jumped back and let out a small "Huh?" before reaching up to his new headgear.

We kept staring, waiting, barely able to breathe.

"He's too old," said Ben. "He just doesn't have the power."

"VAIT!" growled Grigore. He shook his head violently, and the bat wings disappeared. He steadied himself, then took on the same look of concentration. He grunted even harder this time—turning a dark shade of red-purple. But it was starting to work! He shrank, his feet came up off the ground and disappeared into his body, his body shrank into his head, and this time the wings came out large and perfectly formed. His face grew hairy; his nose and his ears took on a pointy quality, and soon he was a small vampire bat, flapping in the middle of the room.

Shane held out his hand. The bat fluttered past Ben and me, and hung itself upside down on Shane's hand.

The bat squeaked a wheezy squeak. Upon closer inspection, I could see that his fur was gone in certain places. His ribcage, heaving from all of the hard work, could be seen clearly through what was left of his hair. He had a small hole on his left wing. Ben bent down and looked through it up to Shane.

The wheezy squeak took on a human quality.

"How's that?" squeaked Bat Grigore.

"Perfect!" I said. "Now, how do we get out of here?"

The two hairy old men stepped forward, along with

the monster that had been stitched together.

"We've got an idea," said the werewolf that had won bingo.

The two old werewolves transformed into their shabby dog forms and raced downstairs—they were filled with energy.

We followed.

RUN!!!

The old green stitched monster, the Director, Ben, Shane, the old werewolves, Grigore, and I gathered just in front of the porch. The sussuroblats were frantically slurping and drooling, and the cheese barrier neared its breaking point. The Nurses turned on the flood lamps and stood on the porch, clubs raised, in case any of the sussuroblats were able to make it over the barrier.

The old green monster stepped forward.

"I will zap them!" he screamed. "You run."

"Zap them?" I asked the Director.

"Frederick came to life thanks to a huge bolt of lightning," said the Director. "And he still retains a small charge that he can use from time to time. I've seen him power a smartphone, but I'm not sure how he intends to create a strong enough 'zap.' Nevertheless, you should get ready to run."

I turned to Grigore, who had changed back into vampire form.

"Are you ready to run?" I asked.

"Ready," he said. "Must. Destroy. These terrible creatures."

"Are you guys ready?" I asked, looking at Ben and Shane. "Do you have all of the cheese?"

"Yep," said Shane. "We collected it from the monsters in the attic."

"All right!" I yelled. "I'll help Grigore along. You guys toss the cheese behind us to slow them down."

The werewolves howled, and a few sussuroblats looked up at us.

The huge old green monster spread his legs apart, unsteady at first.

Then the werewolves began circling around each leg.

Faster and faster and faster.

I could hear a crackle and smell ozone in the air.

"Static electricity," I said, astonished.

"Well," Shane said, "there's one good thing about being a stinky old werewolf with a mangy, dry coat. Charging up monsters!"

Sure enough, the tall green monster began glowing. Brighter and brighter.

"Aaaaaarrrrggghhhh!" He let out a yell that shook the trees. The sussuroblats stopped for a moment.

And then . . .

CRACK!

A huge bolt of lightning blew a hole in the seething pile of sussuroblats, creating a path down the middle of the huge, stunned bugs.

"HURRY!" the old monster screamed, and then fell back onto the ground. The old werewolves licked his face and the Nurses ran down to help him.

"GO! Don't worry about him!" yelled the Director.

We ran through the sussuroblats.

Grigore was slower than I had hoped—I was practically pushing him along.

We hit the forest and headed down the dark, dark road.

Halfway down, we heard them.

BLARFFFF, BLLLLLLARBB, BLURBB!!!

Ben yelled, "They're right behind us!!!"

"Come on, Grigore," I yelled. "You've got to do better. They're going to suck you dry!"

We ran down to the bottom of the hill, and as we burst out of the twisty steep drive and onto the main street, the sussuroblats were practically on top of us.

We turned right and ran for our lives!

Shane and Ben began lobbing hunks of cheese behind us. Most were just bouncing off the drooling field of massive roaches with a small thump.

We ran and ran and ran.

They got so close that I could smell their disgusting breath.

GRELCH! GROLCHHH! BLARFFF! BLURRFF! BLAAAARRRR!

Shane lobbed one more chunk of cheese, and he must have thrown it right into the mouth of one of the sussuroblats, because it exploded with a POP like a squishy, thick water balloon.

"Wooo-hoo!" yelled Shane.

The other sussuroblats slowed down for a second to munch on their fallen friend. But not for long.

"Shoot!" Ben said. "They're still really close."

"Grigore," I yelled, "come on!"

We ran into Belle Aire, a quiet little neighborhood on the south side of town. Jackson Amusement Park was just on the other side.

"All right, lawn-mower master!" Shane yelled to me. "I know this neighborhood like the back of my hand from my paper route, and it's going to take us forever unless we can cut through it! Any smart ideas?"

I yelled, "The Joneses' backyard connects with the Forsythes's. And the Forsythes live on the same street as the park! Follow me!"

Ben threw the last chunk of cheese at the

sussuroblats, which were now just five feet behind us. Another sussuroblat exploded and the gruesome pack of drooly bugs slowed down once more. We were running as fast as we could, but we were still pretty far from the park, even with the shortcut.

We turned left, up the Joneses' driveway. We rushed around their garage and into their backyard.

The sussuroblats followed quickly.

We rushed through a gap in the bushes that lined the backyard, and burst into the Forsythes' backyard.

The sussuroblats slowed down even more as they scraped and scrambled their way through the bushes.

Within seconds, we were on Smith Street. We rushed down the street toward the park.

We were breathing heavily, and out of cheese. But we just had to push as hard as we could and get there.

Grigore was really struggling now as we made the last sprint down Smith Street.

"They're getting really close again," yelled Ben.

"We gotta move!" Shane yelled.

"Grigore," I yelled. "You've got to push it just a little harder."

He shook his head back and forth in an exhausted NO motion.

"We'll just have to pick him up," I said.

Shane, Ben, and I lifted Grigore up. He let out a surprised "Oof!"

"Go, go, go!" I yelled, and we burst forward with newfound speed.

We entered the huge amusement parking lot. Up ahead, we could see the entrance, the rides towering behind it.

The roaches were now only a few feet behind us. I looked over my shoulder to see their teeth flash in the dark.

Their teeth.

Teeth!

"Grigore," I yelled, "spit out your teeth!"

PLOP!

Out came the teeth. They clattered ahead of us toward the entrance for a moment, and then turned around.

ZOOM!

"Whoa!" Shane screeched, and jumped up to avoid the chattering fangs.

They shot behind us and out of the parking lot.

MUNCH, CRUNCH, GRIND!

The teeth made their way through the sussuroblats as they raced back to the retirement home and Grigore's coffin.

The sussuroblats stopped to munch on their wounded. This time, there were more tasty treats, but they were fast eaters—we had to rush.

We ran up to the entrance. We put Grigore down

and shoved our way to the front of the shortest line, annoying everyone.

"Hey!"

"Watch out!"

"What's the big rush?!"

"Old man coming through," Shane yelled. "Respect your elders, people!"

In the parking lot, the sussuroblats screamed and hissed—their snack break was finished.

I threw our passes in front of the sour-looking woman in the ticket booth, and didn't even wait for her to hand them back.

We ran into the amusement park.

"HEY!" she yelled. "Is that old guy okay? I'm not sure he should go on any rides."

We pushed our way through the crowd toward the Gravitron.

Behind us, we could hear screams at the entrance.

"That's disgusting!"

"Are those roaches?"

"I'm outta here!"

The sussuroblats had invaded Jackson Amusement Park.

We ran past the Ferris wheel. We ran past the Haunted House. As we did, a vampire jumped in front of us and yelled, "Welcome to my castle!"

"Vlad?" Grigore asked, confused. "Is that you?"

"Keep moving!" I yelled.

We ran past the bumper cars. The Gravitron loomed in front of us. It must have just finished a ride, because it spun slower and slower.

"Perfect timing," Shane said.

"Let's wait here," I said, panting. "We need to make sure the sussuroblats are right behind us. We have to make sure every last one of them follows us onto the Gravitron."

Shane walked toward the concession stand.

"Wait!" I yelled. "What are you doing?"

"Grabbing some cotton candy," he replied.

"WHAT?!" I screamed. "I said 'wait' not 'hang out.'"

"I don't know why you're so mad," said Shane, walking back. "Isn't cotton candy your favorite? I would have shared."

"I love all carnival food," I replied. "But *we'll* end up as carnival food if we don't stay on our toes."

"Tired," Grigore said. "I'm so tired."

"Just a little while longer, Grigore," Ben said.

Behind us, there was more screaming. We turned around to see the crowd run and the sussuroblats gather in front of us.

"Goooooooo!" I yelled, but Grigore stayed put.

"I . . . just . . . can't," he gasped. "Barely have enough energy to be a bat."

"Grab him!" I yelled.

We snatched Grigore up and ran as fast as we could. As we approached the Gravitron, riders were stumbling off, giggling. And helping them off was . . .

"Karen!" yelled Ben.

Karen, Ben's older sister, was working at the Gravitron!

"Karen!" Ben yelled again. "KAAAARENNN! Don't let anyone else on. WAIIIIIT!"

We jumped into the line, carrying Grigore along with us. We shoved and pushed our way past everyone.

"Hey, no cutting!"

"Ugh, that old man smells terrible!"

"What are you doing?"

We made our way to the front of the line.

"BEN!" Karen screeched. "What are you doing?! I can't just let you cut. Who is that old bum?"

"Hey," said a short, angry girl at the front of the line. "I've been in this line FOREVER!"

Her unibrow furrowed and she gave us an angry scowl.

"Trust me," said Shane, "you are not going to want to get on this ride."

There were more screams, and the kids who were yelling at us just seconds before abandoned the line. The sussuroblats had almost reached us.

"We need to get on NOW!" I yelled.

"I'll explain later," said Ben to his sister, "but you

have to trust me! And make sure all of them are in before you close the door."

"What?" she asked.

But there was no time for any more explanations.

We pulled Grigore into the Gravitron and got as far from the door as we could.

"Grigore," Shane asked as we put the old vampire down, "are you still able to transform?"

The sussuroblats poured through the door, snarling, scuttling, and drooling over one another. They headed straight for the old vampire. Ben, Shane, and I jumped out of the way, hoping that Grigore could make the transformation happen.

Grigore scrunched up his face, grunted, and was able to POP into a bat just as the sussuroblats lunged at him. He fluttered to the center of the Gravitron, and all of the sussuroblats followed, snapping their snaggleteeth hungrily.

The doors closed and Ben, Shane, and I strapped ourselves against the wall.

The monster roaches hissed and snarled at the bat that teased them. Bat Grigore flew just above their drooly mouths, and then shot up higher if any of them pounced. A few sussuroblats tried to scurry over to us, but Grigore would quickly draw them back to the pile by flying right in front of their faces.

The ride slowly started turning. At first, the

sussuroblats didn't notice. When the turning quickened, the sussuroblats were pulled slowly from the center. As much as they scurried and scraped to stay in the center and snap at the bat, they all ended up pressed against the wall. Some had their backs against the wall, their legs flailing wildly.

The Gravitron spun faster and faster and faster.

"Oh, man!" yelled Ben. "Oh, maaaaarrrrrrffff!"

Ben spewed the juicy contents of his stomach all over the two sussuroblats closest to him.

They started to sizzle and smoke.

Shane and I were next, barfing in almost perfect unison. The sussuroblats that had slid over to us began to melt. I'd never been happier to lose my lunch, and only wish I had eaten more before coming to Raven Hill.

The sussuroblats' screams turned to whimpers as they realized what was happening.

Then their whimpers turned to gagging.

They were getting sick!

BAAAAAARRRRFFFF! BLUUURRP! BLAAAAP!

The sussuroblats were barfing all over themselves—and us!

Huge, drooly wads of barf flew around in the Gravitron. Brown barf. Green barf. Bucketloads of barf.

And the barf melted any sussuroblat it touched.

The Gravitron slowed down, and the barf oozed into the center. The sussuroblats that had survived the barf-splosion rolled into the center and were eaten alive by the barf puddle.

Up above, Bat Grigore giggled and let out a wheezy, "YES!"

Steam rose up from the pile of barf and roach parts. Popping and sizzling, every last sussuroblat was coming to a disgustingly stinky end in the Gravitron.

The Gravitron stopped, and we unstrapped our barf-soaked bodies from the wall.

We could hear Karen call out, "Now get out of there!"

She poked her head in and gagged out the words "What . . . happened . . . in here?!"

We stumbled out of the Gravitron, past Ben's sister, and out into the fresh air.

The few kids who hadn't been scared out of the line by the sussuroblats took one look at us and ran.

"Aw, man!" someone called out. "They turned it into a *Barfitron*. GROSS."

"You guys smell absolutely terrible!" Karen said, holding her nose. "Where did those massive roaches go? Why did you want them in there with you? What happened to that old man?"

A small bat fluttered out of the open Gravitron door and circled Karen's head with a squeak before heading off to Raven Hill. She let out a squeal.

"There he is," said Shane. "Safe and sound."

"BEN!!!" she screamed. "I need answers. NOW."

"Sis," he said slowly, swaying on his feet, "I'll tell you everything, I promise. I just need a minute to pull myself together here."

Ben gagged a little, still overwhelmed by the wild ride.

"And you guys?!" she asked. "What do you have to say for yourselves? What just happened here?"

"Look, it's a little complicated," started Shane, "but . . ."

Shane was interrupted by a hiss coming from the open door. One sussuroblat, smoking, but still very much alive, scurried out of the door and to the top of the Gravitron. It let out an angry GRELCH.

"What IS that thing?" asked Karen, a disgusted look on her face.

The sussuroblat turned toward Karen—and jumped right toward her face!

She screamed. Shane and I froze.

Ben steadied himself, opened his mouth, and . . .

WHHHHAARRRRFFFFF!

He spewed all over the sussuroblat . . . and Karen . . . knocking them both backward. The sussuroblat was good and dead by the time it hit Karen's face.

"Oh, man, now that's *talent*," Shane screamed, and gave Ben a high five. Ben smiled and promptly passed out.

Shane laid Ben out on a bench while I reached down to help Karen up. Once she was on her feet, I grabbed the melted sussuroblat at her feet and tossed it back in the Gravitron.

"Oh, MAN!" Karen said. "I think I'm having a nightmare. I should get janitorial to clean this mess up."

She held a walkie-talkie up to her mouth and was about to press the button.

"WAIT!" I said as I grabbed the radio. "I'm not sure that would be a good idea."

"Where are the cleaning supplies?" asked Shane.

Karen pointed past the entrance to the Log Flume to a shack.

"We'll explain everything while we help you clean the Gravitron," I said.

All's Well That Ends . . . Uh-oh

That night, we returned to Raven Hill and found Gordon back to his old, nonbuggy self.

"Took ya long enough," he said.

Leave it to Gordon to insult us for our hard work. I was just happy to hear words coming out of his normal, human mouth.

The Director looked truly happy when he saw us.

"Gentlemen, you did an amazing job," he said. "I can't thank you enough."

The Nurses all came around and shook our hands. By the last shake, our hands were practically crushed.

"Well," I said, "we couldn't have done it without everyone's help."

And it was true. If it weren't for these kooky old monsters coming through in the last minute, our plan would have failed miserably!

"Just wait until I tell the other Directors about you!" beamed the Director.

"Other Directors?" Ben asked.

"We're not the only facility," said the Director. "There are many, many more around the world. There are a lot of residents to tend to, but everyone will be getting a boost of energy with the demise of that sussuroblat pack!"

After the Battle of Raven Hill, Ben, Shane, Gordon, and I came back to volunteer at the home.

Shane continued training the residents in karate.

Gordon helped the Nurses with out-of-control monsters when they needed someone who was quicker on his feet.

Ben's trivia night was the highlight of the week, and he was slowly building up a tolerance to all the funky smells found at Raven Hill.

I worked closely with the Director on special assignments.

It seemed our lebensplasm really was helping the monsters along! As their monster juice was replenished, they all got a little stronger and a little less demented. Except for the zombies. They'd be forever brainless.

Although they still got along great with Shane.

One night, about two weeks after the battle, I was rewrapping a mummy in its pyramid-shaped room.

The Director knocked and entered the room.

"Hi, Director," I said. "I'm almost wrapped up here," I said.

"Actually, I'm the one who's wrapped up," said the mummy.

The Director and I laughed.

"What's up?" I said.

"This is what is 'up,'" the Director said. "I wanted to thank you. I realize that it was a group effort, but we really couldn't have done it without your leadership. Anyone else would have shied away from such a massive task. You took it on without question. Just as we always knew you would."

"What do you mean, you always knew I would?" I asked.

"Perhaps I should let someone else explain," the Director said, and he motioned toward the door for someone to come in.

Rio Vista's lunch lady walked into the room.

"Huh?" I said.

"Hi, Chrees!" she said, and gave me a big hug as if she knew me.

She squeezed me hard. I was completely confused.

"We always knew you had sometheeng special een

you," she said. "Your lebensplasm is strong, you are so smart, and you never brag. You see, I keep an eye out for keeds like you at Rio Vista—keeds who can help Raven Hill out. If there's a keed I think can help, I whip up a special concoction and feed it to them."

"It was her concoction," the Director continued, "along with the volunteer letter that she planted, that drew you to Raven Hill. That combination gave you the feeling that you should help us. Do you remember how angry I was when you snooped around our home? That was never supposed to happen! But that was really the only snag. You were merely supposed to strengthen the residents before the attack happened."

"Wait!" I asked, my stomach suddenly upset. "What *did* you put in my food that first day?"

"It was quite seemple, really," said the lunch lady. "In order to prepare you to do battle with thee sussuroblats . . ."

The lunch lady paused.

"Go on," I said.

"I ground up a few sussuroblats, and put those een your hamburger on thee first day of school."

The Blandburger! That weird crunch! The nasty yellow wad. That funky taste. It was a sussuroburger the whole time!

The room spun around me.

"A sussuroburger," I moaned. "You fed me a sussuroburger?!"

"What's thee problem?" the lunch lady asked. "It's a low-fat protein source."

"It was quite harmless, I assure you, at least once its initial effects wore off," said the Director. "And very necessary to prepare you for our world. I hope you don't take offense."

I stood there for a minute, not sure if I should run... or barf. I was disgusted, but I was also proud that I had been chosen. I had so many questions.

"What about the sussuroblat that attacked the day I told my friends about Raven Hill?" I asked her. "I thought for sure the Director had sent one along to get me."

"That was a deeversion I created," the lunch lady said. "We had just gotten word the sussuroblat army would come that day. I was so happy that you were goeeng to bring friends to fight, and I wanted you to have privacy when you told them. We can't have everyone know Raven Heel's secret, can we? So, I cleared out the lunchroom!"

"Of course," said the Director, "you thought you were fighting the residents of Raven Hill—but your timing couldn't have been better. You were ready to fight something, and fight bravely you did!"

"Thank you for that, Chrees!" shrieked Lunch Lady.

She gave me one more tight hug and left.

"That must have been difficult for you," said the Director.

"Not as difficult as the Gravitron," I said.

"Nevertheless, I have something for your troubles," said the Director.

The Director waved a Nurse in. I think it was Nurse Inx. It was so hard to tell.

The Nurse was holding a package, wrapped up in old newspaper with a silver bow on the top.

"Wow!" I said. "What is it?"

I ripped off one section of paper and saw a lens pointed at the sky. A telescope! Finally, after all of this, my dream had come true! I thought I'd never, ever see the telescope once I paid for all of the Parmesan! I quickly forgot about the sussuroburger.

"That's amazing!" I said, and finished tearing open the package.

"I hope it's what you were looking for," said the Director. "I heard from your friends that it would be the best gift for you."

It wasn't the TRQ92 Super Infinity Space Gazer. It was the TRQ2000—the top-of-the-line model!

"Oh, man!" I said. "This is great. Thank you, Director."

"Call me Zachary," said Zachary.

"How about Director Z?" I asked.

"As you wish," Director Z said. "There's just one small condition for keeping the telescope."

"What's that?" I asked.

"I need you to keep an eye on the sky," he said, suddenly serious.

"Why?" I asked.

"Because the next batch of supermonsters could come from anywhere. We'll need you and the other gentlemen to be on watch. This was just one battle. But we still have to win the worldwide war on these vile new creatures that are after the residents. We will need your help again."

"You can count us in!" I said.

Ben, Shane, Gordon, and I kept volunteering at Raven Hill, and we went about school as if everything was normal. But we knew we could be called into action at any moment.

What monster juice–drinking evil would come next?

About the Author . . .

M. D. Payne is a mad scientist who creates monsters by stitching together words instead of dead body parts. After nearly a decade in multimedia production for public radio, he entered children's publishing as a copywriter and marketer. Monster Juice is his debut series. He lives in the tiny village of New York City with his wife and baby girl, and hopes to add a hairy, four-legged monster to his family soon.